About the Author

First Things First, Fictional love and life resembles reality. It is imperative for me to show how the Lord meets individuals where they are and restores them through His Word for them to become the individuals he predestined them to be.

I am a believer in Jesus Christ, who is the lover of my soul, so much that He gave His life that mine might be saved from eternal damnation. Therefore, His praises shall continually be on my lips. I give Him Glory & Honor for they belong to Him.

I am happily married to a wonderful and handsome man who supports me in all things. He encourages me to stand on the promise that I can do all things through Christ that strengthens me. He is a solid rock, my muse, the second lover of my soul, and the only lover of my body. I adore him. Song of Solomon 3:4, explains how I adore him, by stating "but I found him whom my soul loveth: I held him, and would not let him go." That is Biblical Romance read it for yourself.

Our union has been blessed with two handsome sons, one beautiful daughter, and a Shi-Tzu (dog) we all love and think he is more human than Shi-Tzu.

I have been called to narrate Christian love stories that reflect the greatest love of all time. That love is Christ's love for his bride, the church.

The characters that live these stories don't always start on the right path. Sometimes they fall down, but through the long suffering of the Heavenly Father and their earthly lovers, they find redemption and happiness (in most cases).

Love is patient! Love is Kind!

Chapter 1: Hit-and-Run

She found her one and only love; he found the beat for his heart. Neil and Jessica triumphed over adversity and overcame every obstacle that blocked their way. Now the sky was clear of any clouds that could stop them from living out their destiny.

Camille James sighed as she scrolled over to the rating page on her e-reader and gave the author three stars, and a lengthy written review, for the BWWM Romance novel she completed reading in one setting. She applauded the author for writing a romance book full of angst, twists, and turns that ended in a neat little happily ever after. The three stars were because it was wrapped up too neatly to be believable. However, she would definitely give the author another chance with a different book.

Once she finished the book, she needed to get up and prepare for the next work day—or maybe she would start one more read before turning in. She chose download and laughed at herself, another night alone with her reader.

   She whispered to herself, "I need to get out more, rather than sitting here reading novel after novel and not living my own life. This is not getting me closer to the family that I long for." She knew she needed to be out dating and trying to obtain her own happily ever after. *Oh well. At least I am going on plenty of trips to faraway places with some of the most handsome, wealthy, and caring men ever penned to paper.* She rolled her eyes. *Pathetic.* Camille knew she was and accepted the fact. At thirty-three years of age, reading romantic fiction was how she spent her evenings. Camille had decided a while back that she deserved to relax and drift off to the land of fantasy at night.

   By day, she was the owner of a successful distribution company, In Transit Systems (ITS), with seventy-five employees in Memphis, TN. Camille worked ten to twelve hours a day, six days a week. She put out corporate fires like the chief of a fire department. She was fierce, confident, articulate, and financially secure. Still, it remained true, after six p.m., she was like Levar Burton from Reading Rainbow—in a book. She was taking a trip anywhere other than reality.

A buzz of her mobile device, displaying her best friend Paige Richard's picture, brought her out of her introspective thoughts.

"Hey, Paige, what's up?"

With her normal upbeat voice, Paige said, "Just checking on you . . . what you are doing. Let me guess. You are reading a romance novel written by one of your author-Facebook friends. Who wrote the book for tonight, Camille, LaShawn Vasser?"

Camille laughed. "Whatever, Paige. Surely you did not call for that."

Her tone sly, Paige began. "Well, I actually have a real life date for you. Kevin and I have two extra tickets to a stage play at the theater tonight. Kevin's friend, Benjamin George Adams, has agreed to meet us. So, I have to persuade you to join us."

Since there was only silence, Paige continued. "I promise you will like Ben, and we will have a great time. Now, will you grace us with your presence?"

"Paige, who is Benjamin? Why is he named after dead presidents? What kind of play is it? Who produced the play? What time does it start? I have to get up early in the morning for a 6:30 meeting." The questions rolled out of Camille nonstop, not allowing Paige to respond.

"Whoa—Mille, Benjamin is a friend of Kevin's as I said before. The play is umm . . . I guess urban with a gospel feel to it. The producer is some guy who used to be homeless. Come on, just say yes, do it for me."

"Paige, I will not be attending a play tonight, and with a blind date no less. I'm going to decline on this one."

"Camille, come on, Benjamin is not really a blind date. You two have been at a few of Kevin's political events together."

"Have we been introduced?"

"Not exactly."

"Well, Paige, my friend, the answer is the same. NO!"

Camille was now exasperated. She needed to end this conversation. She had a book she wanted to begin reading before preparing for work.

"Okay, Mille, I see you becoming all tensed and would rather curl up with imaginary people. So what about meeting him next Saturday? We have tickets to another production at the theater."

"Paige! What part of 'I will not be going on a date with someone I have not at least spoken with,' don't you understand?"

"Ok, how about I give you his number, and you can call him?"

"Another negative, Paige. But you can give him my office number, and I will let you know once I speak to him."

"Fine, Mille, have it your way. I wish you would understand you have to live outside of work."

"I do understand that, Paige. That is why you can give him my office number."

"Okay, but do you promise you will allow Karen to put him through, and you will talk to him?"

"Yes, Paige, I promise. Do you need a Color Purple tee tah ta on it?"

"Matter of fact, I do. I will come by your office, and we can do our hand clap tomorrow. I got to run now and meet my man. Smooches."

"Smooches!" Camille replied, ending their call as they did every phone call.

Camille was relieved to disconnect from the matchmaking phone call. She only entertained this Benjamin guy because Paige was one of her dearest friends. Camille vaguely recalled Paige mentioning a guy named Benjamin as one of Kevin's friends. She thought that Benjamin had a girlfriend, but she could not remember. Maybe Camille had nothing to worry about. Most guys would be offended she did not meet on the first request and not call her. One could only hope, but if he did call Camille would go through with her promise to Paige.

Camille and Paige met while attending the Business Institute of Memphis. Camille obtained a degree in Business Management with an emphasis on Project Management. Paige earned a degree in HealthCare Administration. The two hit it off in a study group held at a local bookstore with a coffee shop. They became the best of friends. Over the last few years, they had seen each other through several career changes (including the start-up of ITS), relationships, family tragedies, and so much more. They were both grateful for their sisterhood.

Paige's personality was rough around the edges. While she looked refined and sophisticated, she could go from one to ten in a second. But Camille had nothing but love for Paige because she was loyal. The trust between them was unbreakable. Paige was a true ride or die friend, but often, Camille would have to rein Paige in if she felt provoked by someone.

Camille smiled, thinking about Paige, and returned to her novel. She had to giggle because Paige was correct. She was about to read *A Storm is Coming* by

LaShawn Vasser, and by the end of the first chapter, she knew this one would receive a five-star rating.

The next morning it was a little after eight when Camille made it to her office. She was elated that a local retailer had signed a three-year contract with ITS for their distribution services. Before she could power up her laptop, Karen, her Executive Assistant came on her phone's intercom stating there was a Benjamin Adams on line one. Camille lifted the receiver of her desk phone and said, "Send him through Karen."

Although Camille knew who it was, Benjamin, on the line, she answered the phone in the same professional manner she always did. "Camille James, ITS."

"Hello, Ms. James, this is Benjamin Adams."

"Hello, Benjamin. How are you?"

"I'm well, thanks for asking. I am assuming you know Kevin and Paige gave me your telephone number?"

"Yes. I gave Paige the okay last night. I was expecting your call although not this early. Paige is my persuasive best friend and can get me to do just about anything."

"Well, she could not get you to go out to the play last night," Ben said with a smirk that Camille could hear over the phone.

"Benjamin, you did not want our first meeting to be at one of those gospel-slash-urban plays. The last one I went to, I had Karen, my executive assistant who answered your call, look up the promoter via text for me. It was just that bad. I had to know to whom to give the credit. To top it off, all night I felt like I was on some island and the joke was on me. There was Kevin Michelson, an Assistant District Attorney, laughing out loud at the ridiculous ensemble of cast and hideous dialogue. Not only was he sitting through the ghetto fabulous mess, but was enjoying it more so than Paige. It was just beyond my realm of comprehension. So, Mr. Adams, I did you a favor by not attending it. You would not have appreciated that introduction to me."

Camille paused to allow Benjamin to get his laugh out. She was happy he found mirth in what she said, but she was serious. Poorly scripted gospel stage plays were a pet peeve of hers.

"You know what, Ms. James, we have our first thing in common, and I have a secret to share."

"Really? We are just a couple of minutes into our phone conversation and a secret already?"

"It's nothing major, I promise."

"Okay, so spill it." Camille could not keep her bossy side down, and she hated that. Her last serious boyfriend had said she was too guarded and bossy. Despite what he thought, she did let down her guard and revealed her bourgeois side, which was a plus. There was nothing she could do about being bossy. She was the boss.

"I don't like those plays Kev and Paige are always dragging people to."

"Well, why did you agree to go?" If he didn't want to go, Camille wondered why he said yes. Although she was bossy, Camille did not want a pushover. She bored with them too quickly.

"I tag along because Kevin is my boy, and he is trying to get me out of my normal dating habits. I am trying something new in hopes that I can find the right lady."

Camille thought that was a satisfactory answer and not really a pushover's response.

"So, am I on a *right-lady* phone interview? If so, how am I doing so far?" Camille frowned at herself, did she really ask that? Was she flirting with this stranger? She had to admit that his voice was speaking to her. It was deep and husky and giving her goosebumps. Had it been too long since she had a conversation with a man that was not about business?

"Ms. James, I am the one on the interview. After all, you would not go out with me without a prescreening."

"Touché, but a girl can't be too careful, Benjamin George Adams. By the way, I love your name it is so presidential." *Really, Camille? That was lame.*

"No, I understand. I am happy you stood your ground. I have to respect a woman who makes a brother work for it. If you are as lovely in person as you sound, it will be well worth my effort."

Did he just flirt with me? This brother has game.
Camille blushed. She was positive Benjamin could hear it. Her goosebumps were now sizzling from the heat of his last statement. Benjamin's voice was sensuous, and she could not remain focused on the words, only the sound of his voice. She had to get her mind out of the gutter and steer this ship back to safe, dry land.

"Ummm . . . have you been on many blind dates?"

"I have had more than I would like to admit. However, I can't say that they were official blind dates. I always google her name and check out whatever public social posts, and pictures are available."

"Really? Tell me what you think about my public social media image."

"I did not have time to google you."

"Sure, Benjamin, you did not look me up," Camille said with sarcasm.

"Honestly, Ms. James, Kevin invited me last minute. I said okay then rushed to get dressed. Then he called back and informed me you had rejected me. So I took my broken heart to bed, resigned to call you this morning."

Camille's heart warmed as she listened to Benjamin recap of being turned down. She was regretting not going to the play now. "I did not reject you. I just delayed our meeting."

"Tomato, tomata, Ms. James . . ."

"Well, I gave you my phone number."

"To your place of business, Ms. James."

"Regardless of that, Benjamin, we are now speaking. To prove that it was not my intention to leave you feeling rejected, why don't you text your phone number to 901.789.2345."

"Ok, I'm texting. Whose number is this, your assistant's?"

"Ha. Ha. You are a comedian. That is my mobile number. Ben, can we make an agreement until we meet at the play next week?"

"As long as it does not mean I can't speak to you until then."

"No, just the opposite. Don't look me up, and I will not google you."

"Ok, Ms. James, that is a deal I can make."

"Benjamin."

"Yes."

"Can you kill the *Ms. James*? I get enough of that in business. This is personal, and I want to keep it that way."

"Done, Camille, whatever makes you comfortable. I don't want to have any misunderstandings. This. Is. Personal."

Oh my God! Camille needed to go to morning prayer. Respect was not what this man made her want. If just one conversation with him could have her feeling this way, what would happen when they met? She did not want to ruin any chances that this may blossom into something. That is why she suggested no social media contact. She would live in la-la land for the next week, dreaming he was her Idris Elba. She could not risk taking a look at a profile picture of a man who looked like Urkel, which was her last date. If his looks matched his manly voice, she may lose all her good senses and meet him before the play next Saturday.

The conversation went on for two hours. They talked about ITS, both their families, friends, and religion. They admitted needing to do better about attending church. They both had all consuming schedules. Benjamin did not own his own business, but he was a senior-level executive at the Fortune 500 Company he worked for. They had so many things in common: their love of books, music, art, exercise, philosophy, and both were brought up in the Pentecostal church. Camille could tell his relationship with his mother, Ellen, was at the forefront of his life. He had a cousin who had been raised with him as a sister and was now married with a teenage daughter. She told him about it just being her grammy and dad as she lost her mother at an early age. Since her grammy passed, the only family she had now was her dad. The conversation had Camille smiling and blushing for the duration of the call. She was definitely feeling him. It was Benjamin who had to end the call due to a conference call. He promised Camille he would call her that evening around eight.

That night, and for the next six days, they talked briefly in the morning and for hours at night. Needless to say, Camille had not read one book on her reader since the initial call with Ben. She could not wait to meet him. The anticipation was building with each phone conversation. She was wondering if he was having a battle not to google her. She struggled not to look him up and regretted suggesting the no social media browsing rule. Paige wanted to kick her butt for that insane promise. She told Camille that it was 2015, most people look up a person as soon as they hear a name, and that they were geeks for not already getting it out of the way. Karen helped her feel better about the decision by saying it was sweet, old-school romance—before social media took away the intrigue of meeting someone new. Camille agreed and waited to meet him.

Camille decided to dress simply for the play. She selected a fitted black dress, added sterling silver jewelry, applied light cosmetics, and was out the door. She hopped into her crimson colored SUV, which she loved and would not be trading in for a hybrid of any kind. *Sorry environment!*

While driving to downtown Memphis, she listened to jazz and let her thoughts drift to Benjamin, and all the conversations they had over the last week.

Twenty-five minutes later, Camille was getting out of her truck and saw Paige across the narrow street. She laughed to herself at Paige's attire; the girl was dressed for a black and white event. Paige looked like a black china doll. She was five feet flat, but often wore five- to seven-inch heels. She had mystic brown eyes with a smooth cocoa complexion. Her figure was like a gymnast, which was all genetics because Paige would become winded walking around the block. But there was her best friend, at a simple stage play dressed in a black, strapless, baby-doll, tutu, cocktail dress with, what seemed from the distance like, six-inch platform shoes. She was beautiful but over the top as usual. *Seriously Paige!*

Standing with Paige was Kevin Michelson, Paige's longtime boyfriend. Kevin was biracial, six foot two inches and two-hundred-forty pounds of muscle with dark brown hair, light brown eyes, and clean shaven. Kevin was an Assistant District Attorney for the City of Memphis. With them, stood a dark, handsome man who Camille knew was Benjamin. She could see his presidential air from across the street. Camille glanced at the sidewalk light and saw the *WALK* flash and stepped off the curb. Before she could plant both feet on the street, a speeding SUV came zooming toward her from out of nowhere—actually, it was possible, Camille may not have seen it as she was checking out Benjamin who appeared to be at least six feet tall, and she could not wait to get to him. Before she could react, the SUV was closer, and she felt like a Super Klutz trying to get out of the way. She was petrified of falling in front of Benjamin, as she would not recover from the embarrassment.

Camille heard a crash, and something felt like it was scratching flesh from her face, then a piercing to her abdomen sent heat through her entire being. Her hands began to burn as if she was falling onto hot coals. Was she on fire? She tried to process what was overtaking her. Then it hit her; *it was pain*—violent pain! It took control of her limbs before they began turning cold and went numb. Camille closed her eyes as the numbness took over her body, but before it took total control, the intense pain returned with a vengeance going through her side. Her head started to pound. It was *unbearable*. Her body shut down, and she started to lose consciousness.

Camille struggled to open her eyes and squinted to see Paige and Kevin kneeling at her side. Someone was holding her wrist, taking her pulse; it was Benjamin. She tried to get up, but the pain she felt all over her body did not allow such movement. If Camille was not sorely embarrassed and aching enough, Paige put her to shame by her screaming. Her screams added to Camille's already ringing ears made it feel like fluid was running from them.

"Mille, you okay girl? We called 911. They should be here in a minute. You are about to give me a heart attack! You don't know to look both ways before you cross the street? I know your momma was absent, but didn't your daddy cover that basis with you!"

Great, Paige, let's just spill out Camille's issues while I'm lying in the middle of Main Street, likely dying. The thoughts were going through Camille's mind, but she could not voice them. All she could do was close her eyes and grimace as the piercing pain went from her head to her toes.

Benjamin let go of her wrist and whispered in her ear as she began to fade slowly. "Do not think you are getting out of a date with me. Rest now. I hear the ambulance coming. You will be all better in no time." Camille drifted off under his soothing voice. What a way to go if it was her time!

Downtown Trauma Center

"She has been back there for two hours!" Paige yelled while she paced back and forth in the waiting room of the Downtown Trauma Center. Ben observed his friend Kevin being the patient boyfriend as he tried to soothe Paige with rubs on her back and by helping her take a seat. Paige was a nervous, babbling wreck over her friend. Ben was happy to see this kind of dedication existed between women. Kevin was now a contrast from his Assistant D.A. role that he assumed earlier. He was all business at the accident scene, working vigorously after Camille and Paige left in the ambulance. Kevin pulled out his state identification and took statements from over thirty bystanders along with their contact information. Ben figured it was Kevin's police academy training that allowed him to be sharp enough to know the year, make, and model of the 2013 Ford Expedition that hit Camille. Ben had no clue how Kevin managed to get the license plate number to give to the police because the accident happened so fast. Kevin told Ben that he believed for him to be an effective attorney he needed to know all aspects of the law. So Kevin completed police academy training although he never swore in to be an official officer. Kevin had vowed, the driver who hit Camille and drove off like a coward would be found and charged within twenty-four hours. Now, the three of them waited for a doctor, or any medical professional, to come out and give them an update on Camille's condition.

Ben found himself worrying as if he had known Camille for a lifetime and had googled the possible injuries she could have from the hit-and-run. The injuries could range from minor cuts and bruises to spinal and brain injuries. She had opened her eyes briefly but did not say anything. He could only pray her injuries were not life-threatening. He sent a text to his mother requesting prayer for a friend who had been in an accident. As his mother always said, "Prayer never hurts." She would get their church's prayer warriors to intercede for Camille to recover.

Ben lifted his head as he heard Paige yell, "About time!" He chuckled to himself out of amazement and fear. Paige actually had her hand in the doctor's face pointing at him. The nurse who had called for the family of Camille James was now trying to calm Paige down. Finally, Kevin took her by the arms, and the doctor was able to proceed.

"Ms. James is a fortunate lady. For her to have withstood such a forceful impact, her injuries could be more severe."

Paige blurted out, "Are they severe?"

Dr. Reid swallowed and continued to ignore Paige. "Ms. James has suffered a concussion from the impact of the fall. The right side of her face and both palms have burns and abrasions from when she was dragged down the street. The scans have also indicated possible spinal damage. However, we won't know the severity until the swelling goes down, and we do more tests." Dr. Reid took a breath to watch Paige for any possible outbursts.

Paige remained quiet and allowed him to continue.

"We will keep Ms. James here for the next couple days to continue monitoring her brain functions and her spinal progress." Dr. Reid then looked to the nurse.

"I am Nurse Kay. I will be here until 7 a.m. to take care of Ms. James' healthcare needs, and it would be best if a loved one is near as well. It often helps the patient recover faster."

"Oh, no problem," Paige replied, "I will stay. Is she awake?"

Ben held his breath because that was the question he needed to be answered too.

Nurse Kay stated, "Not at this time. Although we expect her to wake soon."

"Thank you, Nurse Kay and Dr. Reed." They said in unison, and the medical professionals exited through the double doors.

Paige's knees buckled causing Ben and Kevin to reach for her. She sat on the waiting room floor with her head resting on Kevin's chest. She wept and spoke with short breaths.

"Camille has to be alright. She is the only best friend I have. My . . . sister. She has too much going for herself. Her business! Oh, goodness, she has a big client she needs to meet in the morning. I have to call Karen, her assistant. Oh God! This can't be happening."

"Paige!" Kevin spoke firmly to Paige with direct eye contact. "You have to calm down. What is Karen's number? I can call her."

"No, Kevin," Ben interjected. "I can call Karen. I've spoken to her every morning for the last week. You two can stay here. I can go to her office tomorrow and maybe help. Camille has told me about the new account she is trying to bring. It is the least I can do. I mean she was coming to meet me."

Kevin turned to Benjamin, gave him daps, and said, "Thanks, man, that would be great." Then Kevin raised an eyebrow and gave Benjamin an incredulous look.

"You know this is not your fault. We all wanted Camille to come and hang out. She is always working and reading, and we just wanted her to have a night off." Ben remained silent but nodded his head in agreement.

Paige gave Ben a piece of paper that contained Karen's contact information and thanked him. Ben hugged them both and left, content knowing this was a way he could assist. As he walked to his car, Ben could not shake the eerie feeling of the walk he was making. He had made a similar one not too long ago. Just like that time, he felt a connection as if a part of him was in that hospital with her while her life was on the line. Only that time, Lauren, his girlfriend of seven years, died. Ben was praying Camille did not meet the same fate.

****

"Hey there!" Paige said excitedly to Camille. "I am so happy to see you up. How are you feeling?"

Camille tried to speak, and then scrunched up her face and closed her eyes tight. Paige saw her discomfort and began to panic.

"Camille, don't try to talk. I have to call the nurse. She told me to do so as soon as you woke up."

Paige ran out the door in a frenzy. Camille wondered why she was getting the nurse instead of buzzing the nurse's station. Camille looked herself over. Both hands were bandaged. IV's were in her arm, and she wondered what in the world had happened to her. She would wait to question the nurse, but her eyes felt so heavy, and she did not have the strength to keep them open. *Oh, here they come. Great!* Camille wanted to tell the nurse about the pain from the top of her head to her back.

When the nurse and Paige entered the room, Camille made the motions to speak, but she felt vibrations. It felt like an earthquake occurring within in her body. She could hear Paige scream, "What's happening to her?" *Could Paige not feel the earthquake?* It must be the New Madrid fault line that she had always heard would occur in Memphis. Why were Paige and this nurse not feeling it? Then suddenly Camille was plunged into blackness.

The Home of Benjamin George Adams

It was after midnight when Ben made it back home and settled in to call Camille's assistant. He pulled out the slip of paper that Paige had given him and dialed the number for Karen Locke.

"Hello." A sleepy voice answered.

"May I speak to Ms. Karen Locke?" Ben tried to maintain a calm voice, but it felt like a knot had formed in his throat.

"This is Karen, who's speaking?"

Ben cleared his throat. "This is Benjamin Adams, I was out this evening with Camille, Paige Richards, and Kevin Michelson, and I regret to inform you Ms. James was hit by an automobile tonight."

Ben heard Karen gasp.

"Karen, I am praying Camille will be okay. Paige is spending the night with her. They're at the Downtown Trauma Center. Mr. James, Camille's father, lives overseas correct?"

"Yes, he lives overseas and must be notified immediately. He is the only biological family she has."

"I'm sorry, Karen. Paige only gave me your information."

"That's fine. Umm . . . Benjamin, thanks for calling me. I will notify Mr. James. He would be upset if he heard the news from a stranger." Karen paused. "I need someone to tell me Camille is going to be ok!"

Ben did not want to repeat what the doctor and nurse said over the phone, but he had to answer Karen. He tried doing so as calmly and encouragingly as possible. "Camille needs our prayers, Ms. Locke. She took a nasty fall and suffered a concussion. The medical staff won't know more until she wakes up."

Karen let out another gasp, and his heart broke for her. He had known Camille for only a week and felt such a strong connection. But why on earth did he think he should deliver this news to her assistant who, by Camille's own admittance, was a close friend?

"Karen, are you going to be okay?"

Karen struggled to speak but finally said, "Yes. Yes, I will be. Camille is strong and stubborn. She will make it through this."

Ben hoped Karen was right. "That is the right spirit to have, and I agree with you on Camille making a complete recovery. Karen, Paige also wanted me to remind you that Camille had an early morning meeting tomorrow, or later today, considering the time. Will you or another employee be able to handle the client?"

"Yes, she does, but I can handle that."

"Okay, that is great. Paige is staying with Camille tonight. Camille's room number is 318. Hopefully, I will be speaking to you soon with better news."

"Thank you so much for calling me, Benjamin. It sounds like Camille had a date with a nice gentleman."

"I try to be, Karen. Get some rest, and we will stay in touch."

Benjamin disconnected the call and exhaled. He thought about calling Paige, but if she was asleep, he did not want to disturb her. Just as that thought left his mind, his phone buzzed with Kevin's image.

"What's the word, man?"

"You will not believe this, Ben. Paige just called me and said Camille woke up but was having problems speaking. Paige went to get the nurse, and when they returned to the room, Camille had a seizure and lost consciousness." Kevin paused trying to gather his emotions and continued. "They say she is in a coma now and has been taken for some scans and may need surgery. I'm headed back to the hospital to be with Paige."

Ben's heart beat rapidly against his chest as he saw flashbacks of another love. One who was being worked on by emergency respondents trying to shock life back into a beautiful, dying woman. *Not again.* "Kevin, I'm on my way!"

Several Hours Later at In Transit Systems

Karen exhaled as she gathered the signed contracts of ITS's newest client. Camille would be proud that she closed the deal with Specific Designs. Camille had worked on the deal for weeks to bring the up-and-coming retailer for household décor on with ITS. Karen had no doubt that Camille was going to pull through surgery, and her company was going to be just as she left it, if not better. Karen vowed to herself to not let one person or department slack in Camille's absence. Karen and the employees of ITS could not have asked for a better boss or friend. Camille was the catalyst behind

Karen finishing her Business Degree as a twenty-five-year-old single mother. In addition to the tuition assistance from ITS, Camille made balancing Karen's budget less challenging by personally helping Karen financially. To add to her generosity, Camille would babysit Nikki, who was now three years old but still in the terrible two-year-old stage. Camille's babysitting allowed her to complete projects and attend night classes when the babysitter was not available. Tears swelled in Karen's eyes thinking about what life would be like without Camille. The thought was simply too much to bear.

Nikki was the product of a one-night stand with an older man. Karen loved Nikki with her entire heart but regretted her reckless action that night, with a man she did not know. She could not file for child support because she did not know his last name. He had left her in a motel room, with a note and cab fare, after their drinking. That had been her one, and only, time experimenting with cocaine. Karen loathed herself for trying to drown out her pain with alcohol, sex, and drugs. Grateful that her phone ringing took her out of those haunting memories, Karen was relieved to see it was an international call. She could now tell Mr. J. D. James about his only daughter.

****

Benjamin and Paige sat in the waiting room for the second hour of Camille's surgery. The seizure had been caused by a blood clot on the brain. The operation was the only course of treatment to prevent permanent bleeding of the brain, additional clots, and brain damage. Benjamin and Paige had been to the chapel and prayed, now they waited. Ben's mind went back to a similar scene eighteen months earlier, just a couple of floors below in the emergency room.

Eighteen Months Earlier

Downtown Trauma Center

Benjamin stood with his mom, Ellen, and Lauren's mom, Carol, as they heard the somber news regarding his girlfriend of seven years. The doctor was explaining how the blood clot had developed in Lauren's lung and traveled to her heart causing Lauren to have a heart attack. Before medical personnel could assess Lauren, she was gone. Ben could only hear his mom and Carol's wails of grief and sorrow as his very own blood ran cold. Benjamin could only think of the time he had wasted. He loved Lauren, but his focus was on his career. Ben thought they had plenty of time to marry and start a family, and he would not be rushed. Now, Lauren was gone, and suddenly life had new meaning. Immediately, he realized what he let slip away. He now understood time was precious but not promised.

Benjamin spent the next several months helping Lauren's parents with her final affairs and settling a lawsuit against the birth control pill manufacturer that did not disclose blood clots as a possible side effect. The income helped Lauren's family, but no amount of money could fill the void in their lives.

Lauren was on birth control pills because Ben did not want to practice abstinence, so he demanded she take them. He held tremendous guilt over forcing her not to wait for marriage, but not the ultimate act designed for a couple joined in matrimony. To further the insult, he wanted to wait on children when Lauren would have had them willingly, without marriage, but Ben selfishly denied her that as well. For over a year, guilt consumed his every waking moment. He did not consider dating. He stayed close to his mother and Mrs. Carol as they grieved together. After a year of living in the shadows of the past, Benjamin enrolled in grief counseling at Liberty church and began the process of healing. He had grown tired of going through the motions, and a few months after the one-year anniversary of Lauren's death, he decided it was time to move on from grieving to living life again. However, that was easier said than done. While dating, Benjamin found himself with one gold digger after another. What shocked him the most was that successful women were looking for men to retire them after a few dates. He did not realize that, at a certain age, some women wanted to stop working and be pampered. He did not mind doing that for the "Mrs. Right Adams." She had to, at least, offer to give him one child, and these women didn't want to ruin their perfect bodies. That was Ben's desire and prayer now, to be given a second chance at love, family, and marriage. This time, he would do it the right way—God's way.

*****

Bringing his thoughts closer to the present, Benjamin recalled how it was one night just last week that he committed to putting the hurt and pain behind him. He had been sulking at home alone while nursing the one drink he had that evening. Ben declared within himself that he deserved love, and this time he wanted it all. John Legend's song came to his mind as he set in his home office. Ben sang the lyrics to himself—*This time I want it all . . . Last time I didn't know . . . I messed up and let you go . . . this time I want it all . . . this time I want it all.*

The ringing of his home phone stopped Ben's singing. It was Kevin inviting him to see a stage play at the theater. Kevin said he had the perfect young woman to rescue him from his gold-digging dating downward spiral. Ben chuckled at how accurate that assessment was. After Kevin had told him a little about Camille, Ben agreed immediately and disconnected from the call. He anxiously dressed to go on the blind date, hoping it would be the start of something meaningful. He had been honest when he told Camille he went to bed with a broken heart that night.

Kevin often spoke highly of Camille. She appeared to have been a true friend to Paige. And, their conversations over the last week had been the best of his dating life. Camille seemed to be every woman, and he was ecstatic about seeing her in person. While standing in front of the theater with Kevin and Paige, Ben looked to his right as Kevin nudged his side and pointed to the parking lot across the street from where they stood. Ben focused his gaze on a wine-colored SUV then saw an angel step out of it. Camille was beautiful. She looked Native American. From a distance, she had an innocent, elegant style, which was one to behold. She wore a simple black dress. Her light caramel legs were firm and toned. Her shoes were high-heeled. He took a deep breath and walked to meet her as she crossed the street, only a Ford Expedition beat him to it.

****

Benjamin let go of a deep exhale. Paige adjusted in her seat to face him and took his hands in hers. "Ben, Camille is going to come through this." Benjamin squeezed her hands and nodded in agreement.

Across Town

Frankie Jones threw the pillow off his head and tossed the covers off his body. Rubbing his hand down his face, Frankie looked at the clock on his nightstand that read one-fifteen. He had slept the entire morning. He let out a deep groan, got out of bed, and headed to the bathroom. Looking in the mirror, as he brushed his teeth, Frankie sighed as he recalled how he lost control last night. He had gone out for an early dinner with friends and had too much to drink. It had been months since he hung out with the guys and three years since he fell off the wagon. In disappointment, he dropped his head as he could not remember anything after his fifth shot of whiskey. He only accepted the invitation because Brian Andrews, a friend from undergrad, was getting married in three weeks. Frankie knew better than to tempt fate by attending a bachelor party. Frankie thought he would be fine. He knew he had today off from his postal carrier route to sleep in and recover if the night ended late. What was the harm in attending? He sighed. *What's done is done.* He began to recite the serenity prayer.

"God, give me grace to accept with serenity the things that cannot be changed, Courage to change the things which should be changed, And the Wisdom to distinguish the one from the other. Living one day at a time, Enjoying one moment at a time. Accepting hardship as a pathway to peace, Taking, as Jesus did, this sinful world as it is, not as I would have it,

"Trusting that you will make all things right, if I surrender to your will,

"So that I may be reasonably happy in this life, And supremely happy with you forever in the next. Amen."

Frankie turned on the shower and got in, knowing an AA meeting was first on his agenda this afternoon.

Downtown Trauma Center

Camille's eyes widened, and then she suddenly closed them when it felt like the top of her skull was being pulled from her neck. She took her right bandaged hand and went to massage her head. She bolted upright in the bed. *"WHERE IS MY HAIR?"* Camille screamed as loudly as possible, but it only came out as a whisper.

The machine monitoring her heart rate and blood pressure was beeping loud enough to make Camille start banging on the buttons causing pain to shoot up her arm. A nurse came in and explained she was in recovery after brain surgery and must calm down. The nurse turned off the monitor alarms and helped Camille inhale and exhale to slow her heart rate down.

Camille, with tears streaming down her face, motioned to the part of her head that was missing hair. The nurse calmly explained that the right side had to be shaved in order for the doctor to remove the life-threating blood clots. Camille could not believe her ears. She searched her mind to recall what in the world had happened to cause her to need brain surgery.

After long minutes of thinking, she felt like she was running through a maze of memories that were not her own. Camille remembered heading downtown to the play, parking, seeing Paige, Kevin, and Benjamin walking toward her. The SUV . . . The hospital . . . What she thought was an earthquake, and now, opening her eyes with breath in her body. Camille inwardly gave thanks to God for keeping her and protecting her. Camille repented for caring about missing hair when the Lord had spared her life. Camille, with endless tears and a grateful heart, asked the Lord for forgiveness for her sins. She acknowledged Jesus was the Son of God, who died and now was the Risen Savior. Camille welcomed the Lord into her heart and thanked him for saving her soul.

When the nurse came back into the room, she was shocked at the change of the atmosphere in the room; there was now a sense of peace. The patient had gone from throwing a tantrum about her half shaven head to looking like an angel at peace. The nurse looked down at the sedative in her hand and put it back onto her tray. She left the room to allow Camille to rest. The nurse suddenly smiled knowing the presence of the Holy Spirit was in the room. She gave a silent thanks to the master and knew this child of God would be made whole.

Chapter 2: Destiny or Rebound

Benjamin sat with her friends as they waited on Camille to be wheeled to her room from recovery. Paige and Karen had filled the room with balloons. Her clients and employees of ITS sent flowers and edible fruit arrangements. The entire nursing staff had come in to see the suite had been decorated for royalty. Ben held his breath in anticipation as the doors opened and rose to his feet as Camille was wheeled in. Karen and Paige rushed to her, each taking a side, as the nurses stepped around them to set up Camille's monitors.

Ben noticed Camille looked drowsy from the drugs, and he could not miss the bandage on her head. However, none of it subtracted from her beauty. Even in her fragile state, she was stunning. Ben jolted up and in Camille's direction when he heard her slowly attempting to say his name. It came out as a slur, "Ben-jam-en." Ben approached her bed and gently took over propping Camille's head up on the pillows and operating the head portion of the bed as the nurse was instructing. This was to be done to keep the blood flowing properly to Camille's brain, preventing any clots.

When Camille was properly positioned, she whispered to Benjamin, "Y-you do-do not ha-have to be here."

Ben gave an alarming smile and leaned in as close as possible to Camille's face and said firmly, "There. Is. No. Where. Else. I. Would. Rather. Be."

Alcoholic Anonymous Meeting

Frankie took the stand. At six feet three inches tall, he had to lean into the microphone to be heard. "Good Afternoon, my name is Frankie Jones, and I am an alcoholic."

He paused for the crowd to say, "Hi, Frankie," then he continued with his testimony.

"My alcoholism caused me to lose my wife of eighteen years and strained my relationship with my twin daughters. They stopped speaking to me their senior year in high school. I was in denial and convinced myself they were busy enjoying their final year of school. I had to accept reality the day of their graduation. They refused to allow me to attend the ceremony." Frankie gripped the side of the podium and glanced down as if he had a paper he was reading from; only there was none. He looked back up and began again with tears in his eyes. "I was so proud that morning, so proud and sober." He said, with a chuckle, "To see my girls, Dawn and Autumn, graduating as class valedictorian and salutatorian. Imagine my shock and horror when my ex-wife, their mother, Shayla, told me outside the arena that they did not allot a ticket for me. I knew it was because of all the Hell I had put them through. Nonetheless, I could have fallen through the ground as she spoke to me. But crap, I couldn't blame Dawn and Autumn for shutting me out, or Shayla for divorcing me. The height of my alcohol abuse and cocaine addiction was during their high school years. When I would drink and use, I would have total blackouts with no recollection of what I would have done. My girls and wife, sorry, ex-wife, said I never hit them, but I would destroy everything in our house. I would wake up sometimes after binging to find no dining room table or car windows busted out, or my girls' laptops missing or busted up. I was a monster, and they shut me out. Because of my reckless choices and behavior, I spent my girls' graduation day with booze and my best friend, Cocaine. The next day, I woke up beside a young lady who could not have been much older than the twins. Looking at the sleeping, naked frame beside me, I could not remember if her name was Sharon, Karen, or Marion. I had hit rock bottom! I decided then to make a change. I had bailed before she woke up. I left her a wham bam, thank you ma'am note and cab fare. I ran for my life out of that motel room and into rehab where I stayed for three months."

"Over the past three years, I have admitted that I am powerless over alcohol. I have accepted I cannot manage my life without a higher power. I have come to believe that there is a power greater than myself. I've allowed Him to restore unto me sanity. I made a decision to turn my will and life over to Him. He cares for me. I have searched fearlessly into my own moral inventory. I have repented to God and my family. I have made amends. Today, my daughters are juniors at Spellman College and are on the President's list. We have a better relationship than before my addiction. Shayla, my ex-wife, is now my best friend. We attend church together every Sunday morning and have lunch afterwards."

Frankie wiped the tears from his face and made eye contact with his group of peers who struggled with his same demons and said, "It is with great remorse that I say . . . I have been sober for 10 hours. I have fallen, but I am standing again. I will continue to fight for my sobriety."

One Week Later

Downtown Trauma Center

Benjamin and Kevin sat in the hospital's cafeteria over a light lunch. The ladies were helping Camille freshen up, undoubtedly celebrating Camille's pulling through from her surgery. Everyone was thankful that, after a week, her scans showed no signs of swelling, and the spinal x-ray reports came back normal. Although she had mostly slept over the last week, Camille was expected to make a full recovery.

Ben viewed this news as a true miracle from the Lord. He called his mother, Ellen, and gave her the victory report and asked her to thank the church's prayer warriors. Ellen told Ben she would indeed pass the word on. She also hinted that she could not wait to meet this new angel in Ben's life. At that moment, Ben knew, even over the phone, his mom could pick up on his connection to Camille. He said his goodbyes and promised to stop by soon to see her.

Ben was face-to-face with Kevin, who was asking why he felt obligated to be at the hospital every hour on the hour for the last several days. Ben sighed and said, "I don't know, man. It's like a tether formed between us the week we talked over the phone. We developed a routine. A brief check in every morning, and at night we talked for hours. When I saw her get out of her truck that night—I can't explain it—I just know this is where I need to be."

Kevin nodded in understanding and said, "I hear you, man. I just want to make sure you are not seeing this as some type of second chance at redoing things with Lauren. I don't want you using this accident with Camille as a substitute for Lauren, you know, like a second chance or something. You have to admit with the blood clots—it is all similar."

Ben held his hand up stopping Kevin's vomit of words. "First off, I just told you. I can't explain what I am feeling. I will always regret not making the right decisions with Lauren, but she is gone. Camille was stealing pieces of me from conversations alone. When I saw her that night, she was breathtaking. She is the most beautiful woman I have ever seen. And despite her half-shaven head and bandaged body, I still want to be near her. I can't leave her now. When Camille was hit by that car, she was coming to meet me. When I knelt beside her at the scene something just clicked in me. Man, I can't explain it, but I am here, and I know this connection I feel is not me substituting Camille for Lauren."

Kevin sighed and attempted to speak, but his cellphone alerted him of a text.

"Look, Ben, this is Paige. Mr. James, Camille's dad, is at the airport, and I need to scoop him up. Do you want to ride or stay here?"

Ben opted to stay with Camille. He certainly did not need any more awkward moments with Kevin, and he wanted to be alone with Camille. Benjamin knocked on the hospital door lightly and pushed the door open when he heard a light voice say, "Come in."

He walked eagerly into Camille's room and to her side. He bent down and gave her a gentle kiss on the forehead. "I am so happy to see you awake. You gave us quite a scare there."

"I am sorry, Ben. You have been so patient. This has been a horrible beginning to a friendship. Not to mention, the worst first date ever."

"No such thing. It has been full of adventure, suspense, and is still going strong."

Camille gave him a look of bewilderment and tried to laugh, but the throbbing in her head would not allow it.

"Why are you laughing, Ms. James?"

"You are corny, and quit the *Ms. James.*"

"I guess that was lame." Ben shared the laugh with Camille.

"Seriously, Ben, thank you for staying and making sure I'm okay. I promise when I am all better, I will give you a call for a redo. You have a life and a career to get back to. I don't want to keep you any longer."

Ben looked at Camille with confusion. "Camille, I don't want to wait for a redo. I want to be here. I want to continue to get to know you without any breaks."

"Ben, I am not myself. I have half my head shaven, and the doctor says it could be six to eight weeks before my speech and motor skills return to full capacity. I have made some personal and spiritual vows while being here. It would not be fair to you. I don't know who I am anymore, or what's next for me. Please, Ben, I can call you to chat about my progress, but I don't want you to feel like you need to give me some kind of charity friendship because I could not cross the street."

"Camille, I want to continue to see you. I can work from anywhere. I have my laptop bag and my two mobile devices with me. I have not missed one call or conference meeting in the last week. I want to share in your recovery, not out of charity or pity, but because I care for you. You are beautiful on the inside and out, bandages and all. Besides, you just had brain surgery a week ago, and you are speaking clear enough to push me away. So, I don't see anything fragile or confused about you. Please allow me your friendship. I too have been working on my relationship with the Lord. Maybe we can do it together." Ben gave Camille the most desperate and pleading look he could manage. He was serious about not experiencing any breaks in getting to know her.

Camille's stubborn will broke as she looked at Ben's pitiful expression. "Well, Benjamin, I can see why you are successful. It's very hard to say no to you with that kind of sales pitch."

Quickly his face broke into his charming smile, and he scooted a chair next to her bed. "Now, give me the scoop on your father. I don't want him to kick me out when he arrives."

Camille smiled. "Have you heard of the saying 'what you see is what you get' ?"

Ben confirmed, yes, with a head nod.

"Well, Jacob Darius James is the opposite. He is one to observe and only speaks when there is pertinent information to request or demands to be given out."

Ben jerked his head backward and raised an eyebrow. "Really?"

"Really. But don't look like I just said my dad was some big mean guy. He simply does not deal in nonsense. There you have it, the 411 on my daddy."

"Camille, is that all the information you are sharing?" Ben said. Wrinkles creased across his forehead.

Camille giggled at the perplexed look Ben was giving her.

"Camille, seriously. I barely got you to agree to let me stay. I don't want anything messing up my opportunity of getting to know you."

Camille could see his sincerity and felt it was a little intense after a couple of weeks knowing one another. Not even considering she spent the last week in and out of consciousness. She tried to move the conversation away from their budding relationship. She could not think of where they were headed, under the influence of morphine. Camille tried her best to speak clearly. "Ben, we practically just met. We have not been on an actual date. There is no need to be tense regarding my father. I will just introduce you as a friend of Kevin's. I will even say you are a Good Samaritan and have not left my side." Camille tried to offer a genuine smile but reached for her forehead with her bandaged hand as her smile turned into an anguish-fueled grimace.

Benjamin jumped to his feet and rubbed her forehead with his left hand and lowered her bandaged hand with his right. He spoke softly to her.

"Camille, are you okay? Did cutting me down to size give you a headache?" Camille rested her head back on the pillow and closed her eyes while Ben slowly massaged her temples. Ben begin to hum a song, then softly sang with a melodious voice. Ben's touch and voice became a sedative to Camille as the headache began to recede.

Camille focused on the lyrics he was singing softly in her ear while sitting on her hospital bed holding her hand. The lyrics were clear and direct to Camille. Benjamin George Adams could not be cut down to size nor was he backing off. Camille asked the name of the song and artist. Ben informed her it was "All I'll Ever Ask" performed by Freddie Jackson on a Najee CD. Camille allowed herself to fall into slumber under the rapture of Ben's voice.

Love means so many different things
But you're all that matters
and this is all I'll ever ask of you
Tell me your dreams, so they can be mine too let
me be there to help them come true
tell me your fears, when you feel afraid
Come to my arms let me rock them away

That's all I'll ever ask,
that's all I'll ever ask, that's all I'll ever ask
of you
Come to my shoulder when you need to weep
Wake me up, when you cannot sleep
Talk to me, when you want to be heard
be silent with me, when you can't say a word
That's all I'll ever ask, that's all I'll ever ask
that's all I'll ever ask,
of you

When Ben saw that Camille was asleep, he kissed her on the forehead. As he was rising, the nurse entered to change the IV bags. He exited quietly and headed to the chapel and was happy to find himself alone. He knelt on his knees at the altar of the chapel and prayed.

"Heavenly Father, I come to you with a grateful heart. Thank you for sparing Camille's life. Thank you for bringing her into mine. Thank you for another chance Lord, another chance to say I am sorry for the sin in my life. I am sorry for seeking after earthly things instead of seeking your will. I accept you into my life right now Lord, because you have answered my prayer. You have shown me my missing rib. Father God, I was so torn with guilt over how I never committed to Lauren. Her death left me shattered with a wounded spirit and condemnation. I give that over to you Lord. I know, just like Adam knew with one look at Eve, the woman you created for him, that Camille is bone of my bone, flesh of my flesh. Father, I need your help in being who she needs me to be. Guide me so that she can feel this is destiny and not a rebound. Father, you said in your word 'It is not good for man to be alone.' Your word also tells me, 'He who finds a wife finds a good thing, and obtains favor from the Lord.' I am ready to 'Seek first Your Kingdom and Your righteousness, so all these things will be given to me.' Lord, I am ready to drink from the well that never runs dry. Lord, I know Camille is my missing rib. Show me how to care for her and in your timing she will know this is right. Show me how to nurture her back to the fearfully and wonderfully creature you made. In Jesus' name, Amen."

****

Paige & Kevin sat in a traffic jam on their way to the Metro Airport. The ride had been a silent one as they listened to soft Jazz by Ben Tankard. Kevin broke the silence. "Paige, I called my parents and told them about Camille. I told them coming down next weekend was up in the air."

Paige turned and looked at Kevin, "What did they say?"

"They said not to worry. We could come down anytime, and they were praying for Camille."

Paige smirked. "Was that your dad? I don't believe your mom actually cares."

"Paige, that is not fair. Mom was concerned. I really hope, during the next trip you, and Mom could come to terms and be friends, or at least friendly with one another."

Paige rolled her eyes and lifted her chin up to meet Kevin eye to eye. "Kevin, I know you are not saying it's my fault that Julia and I are not friendly. Need I point out that as a black woman dating a biracial man, I expected if I was going to be judged by anyone in your family that it would not be your *black mother*! I mean your dad is a judge, and he does not make assumptions of others before getting to know them." Paige's neck started to twist as she continued. "Your mom did not give me a chance before writing me off as some trifling gold digger."

Kevin tried to interrupt the tirade he saw Paige was about to begin. "Honey please!"

Paige raised her hand to halt the interruption. How Kevin wished the traffic would start to move again.

"Kevin Michelson!" Paige screamed, to bring him out of his daydream. She started a count on her fingers. "Number one, from the moment your mother met me, she has done nothing but criticize what I am wearing and my hairstyles. Heck, the woman called me common to my face. Number two, she tries to get under my skin with the shade she throws at me. It's insulting! Where we are, is of no consequence for your so called 'Elegant and Refined Momma.' I swear, Kevin, if it was not for you and your sweet dad, I would have snapped on your mom months ago."

Kevin jumped in. "Paige, that's it, you do snap. You both snap at each other all the time. It's like you two are competing for who can be more hood." Kevin immediately regretted that statement.

Paige rolled her eyes and bit down on her lip, then looked at him with venom. "Kevin! You seriously better not be calling me hood. I may not have come from high society like you, but I am far from the hood, sweetheart. No one will make me feel that I haven't achieved everything I have through hard work. I cannot believe you would say that to me."

"Paige, I did not mean it that way. I am just saying, you don't have to give in to her antics. I admit my mom is judgmental and can be superficial at times. However, what she thinks of you will not deter my love for you. So next time we go, just don't be so willing to go down with her."

Paige was passed furious and said, "Kevin, you really need to have this conversation with Julia Michelson. She needs to know, and I need to know you will not allow her or anyone else in your family to disrespect me. You pursued *me*. I have been nothing but open and honest with you. Now, if you want to keep me, it is your job to keep your beast of a mother out of my face. I am warning you; if she continues to come at me like she has been, like she is all that, as if I am some common chicken head, then hood it will be!"

"Fine, Paige, I'll speak to Mother."

Kevin gave up this battle. It had been a stressful forty-eight hours, and he had no wins when Paige's sister from the hood persona, *Raige*, was out. Finally, the traffic started to move, and he could not wait to get another person in the car to break the tension between him and Paige.

As he drove, only the sounds of Ben Tankard streaming through his car's speakers could be heard. Paige had shut him out. He had to admit that Paige was right, and he had to set his mom straight about her attitude. He intended to be with Paige permanently. He already purchased the engagement ring. His mom would have to accept Paige and stop pushing her buttons to have her acting like a hood rat. Paige could go from a sharp, classy woman to her ghetto persona, nicknamed Raige by Camille. He knew Paige had this self-preservation persona because of her childhood. She was left abandoned in the apartment with her mother's corpse after she overdosed on heroin. Paige spent three days alone at the age of six, caring for herself and her dead mother. When Paige had been found by the authorities, she was clean, fed, and the apartment was spotless. Apparently, Paige had been taking care of herself and her drug-addicted mom since she was four or five years of age. She was taken in by an aunt who lived in the same housing projects where her life was full of hurt, rejection, and abuse. It would have been easy for Paige to stay in the projects and continue the cycle of poverty, but she didn't. Instead, Paige did the exact opposite. She had been on her own since she was eighteen. Leaving her aunt's home, who was only interested in the monthly food stamps and state check she received while Paige was a minor, Paige worked two jobs for years and put herself through college. She was now the director of a health insurance agency. Kevin loved Paige with all of his heart.

He reached over, grabbed her hand, and kissed the back of it.

"Paige, I am sorry. I will deal with my mother, just be patient. I love you so much."

Paige's anger broke. She gave him a smile and leaned in to kiss him.

"Ok, Kevin, I don't want to fight anymore. I am worried about Camille, and I should have never begged her to come to the play. She would have hated it anyway. I know what she finds entertaining, and she would tell you an urban stage play was not the genre she preferred. She probably would have left during intermission, citing a headache."

"Paige, this is not your fault. Things happen in life; unexpected circumstances come into play. Besides, Benjamin is feeling Camille."

Paige looked shocked. "Really? They haven't had much time to get to know one another."

Kevin hunched his shoulder. "Ben told me earlier he felt a connection with her. The two of them spoke on more than one occasion before the date. He said 'they had a tether that bound them.' He dang near ripped my head off when I questioned him why he felt the need to stay by Camille's side."

Paige smiled and held Kevin's hand tighter. "Well, I guess we will see what happens."

Chapter 3: Introductions & Reunions

Downtown Trauma Center

"So, it's settled," Ben stated to Karen. "I will come into the office with you Monday. You can show me around, and I can be the liaison for you and Camille as she recovers."

"If that is what Camille wants, then I'm fine with it." They both turned and looked at Camille who was playing with Nikki and her toy Shopkins on the bed.

Camille glanced up. "We have no other choice, Karen. Benjamin is a senior vice president at a Fortune 500 company, and he is volunteering. I don't want you weighed down with your job and mine. Besides, someone has to take care of our princess, Nikki." Camille held out her arms to Nikki for a hug although it caused her pain. Hugging her god-niece was worth it.

Benjamin sat observing the trio as they played with the little vegetable toys. Nikki pointed to him and said, "This one is Chloe. She is a cauliflower, and she likes leafing around. This one is Silly Chilly, and he is a pepper that eats hot dogs. My favorite is this one, Juicy Orange. She keeps juicy secrets—shhh." Nikki put a finger to her mouth to quiet everyone down.

Ben laughed, little Nikki was three going on thirty. He asked, "Is that all of the Shopkins?"

"No, sir. There is Dipping Avocado and Corny Cob, but Momma says I have to stop pulling clips for acting bad in daycare before I can get them."

Ben winked at Nikki. "I have a feeling you will be getting them all soon."

"Really!" Nikki screamed.

"Yeah, really!"

Nikki turned to her mom and Tee-Tee to tell them what Ben said. Ben was amazed at the striking resemblance between Camille and Karen. It was as if the two had the same demeanor only their skin tones were different. Camille more a milk chocolate while Karen was a smooth hazelnut. Their interaction with one another was more of familial than friendship or boss and employee. He caught himself before he asked if they were sure they were not related.

A knock on the door made all heads turn, and Camille gave a softly slurred, "Come in." Seeing J. D. enter, she managed to squeal out, "Daddy," as he walked toward her hospital bed with nothing but love in his eyes.

"Baby girl," he whispered as he lowered his lips to Camille's forehead. Her eyes sparkled with tears. It had been so long since Camille had last seen him. J. D. doted on her while she assured him she was doing better and progressing faster than the doctor and specialists predicted.

After ten minutes of conversation between just the two of them, Camille finally said, "Daddy, let me introduce you to my friends."

J. D. looked around and said, "Pardon my rudeness, I just did not expect to see my baby girl this way." Everyone expressed their understanding.

Camille began with Karen. "Daddy, this is Karen Locke, my assistant, and friend, and this little Shopkin is Nikki, Karen's daughter and my god-niece."

J. D.'s expression was awestruck. It was as if he had seen a ghost. The entire room noticed the change in his disposition as J. D. reached out his hand and said, "Nice to meet you, Karen and little Nikki."

He scanned them both over from head to toe as if he knew them. Karen, in an effort to break J. D.'s stare down, said, "Nice to meet you, Mr. James. It's a pleasure to put a face to a name."

"Yes, it is, but please everyone, call me J. D." J. D. gave an awkward smile and said hello to Benjamin as Camille introduced him as a friend of Kevin's. It was not lost on Benjamin that she did exactly what she informed him of earlier. Nonetheless, he gave a manly handshake to J. D. James.

"Well, Daddy, you know Paige and Kevin."

"Of course I do, thanks for the lift, and the update on Mille although I still was not prepared."

Kevin said, "No problem that is what friends are for. How long do you think you will be in town?"

"I don't know, but as long as it takes my baby to be well."

They all turned to look at Camille, but she had drifted off to sleep. J. D. looked concerned. "Is this normal?" he asked. He was expecting Paige or Karen to answer, but Benjamin started.

"Yes, she was experiencing some pain earlier, so the nurse gave her pain medicine. It normally keeps her out about three or four hours."

J. D. was caught off guard by Benjamin responding. He scratched the side of his head. A look of bewilderment was clearly evident on his face. *Who was this man to Camille? She introduced him as a friend of Kevin's. Why would he be answering questions?* Camille had not mentioned a special man in her life. *Had she?* He turned to Benjamin and asked, "Exactly . . . what is your relationship with my daughter?"

Benjamin cleared his throat and said, "I am a friend, sir."

Karen immediately said, "Benjamin is also helping with some of Camille's responsibilities at the office while she recovers."

J. D. said firmly, "I see. Well, I am going to my hotel for a shower and a little rest. I will be back in the morning unless she wakes and needs me. I will catch a cab."

Kevin interjected, "J. D. that won't be necessary. I am happy to take you."

"No, Kevin. I need the time alone, thank you." He exited the room.

After J. D.'s departure, everyone in the room exhaled. Karen spoke first. "Geez, he is intense over the phone, but my goodness . . . he was looking at me like I was the one who hit Camille with the SUV."

Paige rubbed Karen on the back and said, "J. D. is always intense, don't worry about it."

"Okay, I will try not to, but can I ask a favor? A coworker dropped Nikki and me off. Can we catch a ride home with you and Kevin?"

Kevin said, "No problem, but I have to stop at the office to check messages and see if there are any leads in finding the perp that hit Camille."

"No problem," Karen said.

"Well, you three go ahead," Paige stated. "I will stay here with Mille."

Kevin frowned. "Paige, you have stayed the last two nights, I thought we could—"

Benjamin cut into the conversation. "I'll stay."

"Ben, I can't ask you to do that. You have done more than enough. You need rest before you go to the office tomorrow," Paige explained.

"No, I am fine here. When Mr. James returns, I will leave. Please, you all go, I have it covered here."

Kevin pulled Paige in an obsessive manner that made Karen frown, but she said nothing. She gave a friendly wave good-bye to Ben and said, "See you in the morning."

Little Nikki pointed a finger at Benjamin with one hand and with the other hand on her hip said, "Take care of my Tee-Tee, Mr. Ben."

"You got it, Little Ms. Shopkin." Benjamin kneeled down and gave Nikki a handshake to seal the deal.

Three Months Later

Camille sat up, feeling slightly out of breath from tying her shoes. She was waiting on Benjamin to come for their evening walk. She could not believe the turn her life and circle of friends had taken in the last few months. First, she hated to admit to herself, but Benjamin was taking up more room in her heart, mind, thoughts, and soul than she felt she could make room for. However, she was grateful for how he stepped in at ITS and had aided Karen in running the company as if she was still there. When she tried to compensate him, he declined saying he did not need any more income to pay taxes on.

Then there was Karen—running into Frankie Jones at Kevin's office, the day he and Paige were taking her home from the hospital. Frankie was the postal courier for the District Attorney's office, and apparently, the one-night stand that fathered little Nikki. The paternity test was back, and Frankie was, as Maury Povich would say, "indeed 99.99%, the father." At first, Karen was unsure of how she wanted to proceed, but

Frankie said he wanted Nikki to know his family. His twenty-year-old twin daughters, who were in college, and his ex-wife, who was his best friend.

Camille shuddered at all the drama in her world. Immediately, her thoughts went to Paige and Kevin, and their tumultuous trip to Atlanta that landed Paige in jail for twelve hours for assaulting Mrs. Michelson, Kevin's mom. Fortunately, Kevin and his dad got Mrs. Michelson not to press charges. No one had given Camille the details because they did not want to hinder her healing, but how could being in suspense and worrying, help? She shook that off as her mind wandered to her father. J. D. had been there for the past three months, but he seemed on edge like something was bothering him other than her health. Camille knew her father and knew there was more. What could she do, but wait until he was ready to open up and talk to her. Until then, she would focus on the doctor's orders, and do her daily mental and physical workouts, so she could get back to business. Just then her doorbell rang, and a smile spread across her face for she could feel Ben's presence near. She walked as fast as she could with her light limp to greet him.

****

"Hi, Cam." Ben greeted Camille with his new moniker for her as he leaned down and gave her a kiss on the temple and squeezed her tight.

"Hi, handsome." Camille returned the hug one hundred fold.

"Is my girl ready for our walk?" Ben asked as he pulled back from her to peer down her body. She was becoming more beautiful every day. There was barely a scar left on her radiant face. Benjamin, who never cared for weaves, thought Camille's looked as natural as her own hair. She was the most beautiful woman he had ever had the pleasure of viewing.

"Earth to Benjamin," Camille said. "I am ready for our walk. Let me get my water bottle, and we can go."

"Um . . . okay." Benjamin wondered when being in her presence would become easier. She always made him drift off thinking of her beauty.

Thirty minutes into their walk they had hit one and a half miles and the conversation was flowing smoothly. Ben turned to Camille and said, "I want you to come to Sunday dinner to officially meet my family."

Camille blushed. "Ben, I have met your mom. Dare I say, we are friends. Mrs. Ellen is one of the most beautiful women inside and outside that I have ever met."

Ben warmed at that comment. "Thanks, Cam, but I am ready for you to meet my aunt, uncles, and grammy."

Camille gave a smile that spread across her entire face. "Really, Ben, so soon? I mean you have been a lifesaver for my company, and a caretaker for me, personally. However, outside of that, you don't know the 100 percent Camille James. You sure you want to introduce me to the extended family?"

Ben stopped their walk, grabbed Camille's hand, and looked her in the eye and said, "I. Have. Never. Been. More. Sure. Of. Anything."

Camille gave an embarrassed chuckle and raised up on her tiptoes, kissing Ben gently on his lips and said, "Yes, I would love to meet them."

They proceeded back to her apartment completing the two-mile journey in forty-five minutes. It wasn't lost on Ben that it was their best time yet. He also cleared his thoughts of what his body wanted to do after that wet kiss Camille bestowed upon him. Things were heating up for them.

Kevin's Downtown Condo

"Paige, I am trying to understand why I had to convince my *mother*, of all people, not to press charges against my girlfriend. Please give me something that can help me understand what would cause you to freaking flip out like that."

Paige, who was sitting on his couch, did not speak or look Kevin's way. Kevin was close to the edge of losing it on Paige and continued to question her.

"Who assaults their future mother-in-law?" Kevin shouted at Paige. She had sat stubbornly staring into space like a zombie until the last phrase was yelled into her face.

Paige whipped her head around. To Kevin, she looked like the girl from *The Exorcist*, as fast as her head twirled in his direction. He braced himself for her hood persona.

"Kevin, what do you mean future mother-in-law? I do not have a ring on my finger, and the way your mommy dearest treats me—and you and your father allow her to—I don't know that I want a ring from your spineless ass!"

Kevin threw his hands up. *Here we go, and Paige from the hood is out.* He asked her as calmly as he could, "Why profanity, Paige?"

"Why profanity!" Paige screamed until her voice became hoarse. "Because there are no dignified words to articulate how fed up I am of you trying to get me to be a doormat for your raggedy momma." Paige was up and standing toe to toe with Kevin. "That so called lady of sophistication . . ." Paige made quotation marks with her fingers as she said sophistication. "Had the nerve to tell me I was not good enough for you. You want to know why?"

Kevin was sure that was a rhetorical question, so he remained quiet.

"I am not good enough for you because I came from a drug addicted whore. She went on to say that whore, which is my mother mind you, did not have enough sense not to overdose on heroin. Then the great Mrs. Michelson told me the apple had not fallen far from the tree and, that I am nothing more than a gold digging whore like my pathetic mother. To follow up those insults, she spits in my face. So tell me, Mr. D. A., how do I respond to that?"

Kevin knew that too was rhetorical. He wiped the sweat from his forehead and tried with all his might to keep his anger in check. He had no clue his mother could be so cruel. He wanted to reach out and comfort Paige, and tell her it was ok to stop this closing argument in her defense. Shamefully, he had lost the ability to speak or move, so he just stood listening.

"I will tell you how I responded! I put my foot up her—" Paige caught herself before more profanity slipped out. "Let me say the appropriate word for you, derriere. I wanted to physically kick her into the next century. Then I proceeded to snatch every extension out of her bald head. I slapped her so hard, her glued on eyelashes went flying across the room. I grabbed her by the neck making that Tiffany of New York necklace snap, and I would have choked the very life out of her had you and Mr. Michelson not come in. I was Hell bent, excuse me . . . I was *determined* to allow Julia to make acquaintance with my whore of a mother in Hell! Where she is surely on her way. Now, you still want to give me a ring?" Paige asked sarcastically.

Kevin stood there stunned and speechless.

"Oh wow, Mr. District Attorney," Paige sneered. "No rebuttal? Well, there is no need because I rest my case and withdraw from this tired-ass relationship. Oops, there is that hood persona again. Forgive me, Kevin, let me rephrase to your legal terms. This relationship is no longer giving me what I need to be the best person I was destined to be. Therefore, I would like you to lose my freaking number and never speak to me again." Paige grabbed her purse, retrieved her cell phone, and called a cab. She informed the cab company she would be waiting outside the Mississippi Waterfront Condos.

Kevin was left standing in place, speechless, as she slammed the door.

Capriccio Grill, Peabody Hotel

Frankie sat in the upscale restaurant with Shayla, Dawn, and Autumn drinking ginger ale. He was more nervous this day than he was when he received the paternity results. This was the first time all the leading ladies in his life would meet, and he was nervous as all get out. He had spent the last few months with Karen and Nikki and loved his little girl completely. Karen was beautiful and warm, and he had yet to figure out what prompted her to do drugs and have a one-night stand. She was nothing short of responsible.

"Daddy!" Dawn called out breaking into his thoughts. "Are you here with us? You seem nervous."

Frankie smiled warmly at his more caring daughter and said, "Yes, Pumpkin, I am nervous. I want this all to go smoothly."

"It will, Daddy!" Dawn and Autumn both exclaimed.

Autumn held her dad's other hand and said, "I can't wait to spoil my little sister."

"Thanks, girls. I knew I could count on you." Frankie lifted one of each of their hands and gave them each a kiss on it. Then Frankie turned to Shayla and asked, "What are you thinking, sweetheart?"

Shayla sighed, "I don't know how I feel, Frankie. We were married so long. Now, we are in a good place. I just don't know where I will fit in."

Frankie had a feeling that she felt some kind of way about his new family. He wanted to ease her into this transition. "Shayla, you are the mother of my girls and my best friend." Frankie reached over the table and grabbed her hands to reassure her.

Shayla had tears in her eyes as she held tightly to his hand and said, "Karen is the mother of your other daughter. What is to stop her from becoming more?"

That statement tore at Frankie's heart. Shayla had never given any indication that she wanted more than friendship. He understood why she didn't want to be more than friends. He had put her and the girls through so much during his addiction. He wanted to comfort her and tell her they had a chance, but he could not as Karen was taking up more room in his life, heart, and mind.

Before he could say anything, he heard a high-pitched voice scream, "Daddy, we are here!" Frankie rose from his chair and met his little Shopkin in the middle of the restaurant, giving her a twirl just the way she liked. Nikki held on to his neck and smiled showing all teeth and gums. She had lost her two front teeth in an accident.

Karen came rushing behind them and apologized. "Sorry, she was so excited, I could not keep up."

"No problem," Frankie replied. "I'm happy to see Miss Shopkin here too. How are you, Karen?" Frankie held Nikki in one arm and pulled Karen to him, giving her a lingering kiss on the forehead.

Karen blushed and pulled away as she felt three sets of eyes zoom in on them with intensity. When Karen stepped back, Frankie turned to see what had alarmed her and remembered Shayla and the girls were with him. Karen and Nikki did this to him. Their presence took him to another place, a place of hope and promise.

Frankie could not explain it. Maybe it was just gratitude toward Karen for being responsible and raising Nikki to be this bright little girl. He had learned that Karen did not once think about aborting his Miss Shopkin. Instead, she put herself through college while progressing in her career. He was in awe. With the one night they shared in creating Nikki, he could not have dreamed she was a responsible, educated lady. Her beauty and grace were an added bonus. He was totally captivated by her and his daughter. However, this was not just their new little family. He had to begin the blending of all his ladies. By the look on the girls' and Shayla's faces, he was not sure it would be a smooth one. He took a deep breath and led Karen, in front of him, with his hand on the small of her back toward the table. Nikki laid her head on his shoulder as he held her. When he made it to the table, Dawn and Autumn both stood and then nudged their mother, who had a look of defeat all over her. When Frankie approached, he introduced Karen first to his daughters and Shayla. The girls both greeted Karen with a hug.

Autumn grabbed Nikki and said, "Hi, we are your big sisters."

Shayla shook Karen's hand and said "Hi, nice to meet you." Then she excused herself to the restroom. Karen had no idea on how to feel or what to think about her sudden departure but focused her attention on her daughter and her big sisters. Nikki was overjoyed with having twin big sisters. She started chatting with them as if she had known them all her life. Dawn and Autumn were under the Shopkins spell in less than ten minutes. However, after thirty minutes, Dawn brought up the elephant in the room saying she had to check on her mom, who had not returned. Frankie asked Autumn what she thought was going on with Shayla.

Autumn shrugged. "Dad, I don't think she can handle this setting." She said this while using her hand to motion to Frankie, Nikki, and Karen.

Frankie was flabbergasted. "What do you mean this setting? Shayla knew the purpose of this lunch was for you all to meet Karen and my baby girl."

"Dad!" Autumn exclaimed, "Yes, she knew, we all knew, but none of us expected you three to seem like a family. Where I am tickled pink to have Nikki, and you too, Karen, in our lives, Mom may need time to adjust. That's all."

Karen understood. She leaned into Frankie and said, "Maybe I should go. Autumn is right, from everything you shared with me about Shayla, I don't want to ruin her afternoon."

"I'll have none of that. Shayla and I are friends and nothing more." Although he and Karen had not made anything official between them, he was certain she was his future.

Karen beamed with pride. She was elated how Frankie had stood up for her and Nikki. She grabbed Frankie's hand, looked over at Nikki, and said, "Nikki, Mommy needs to leave and take care of something. Can you stay here with Daddy and your sisters?"

Nikki nodded and said, "Yes, ma'am."

"Okay, then it's settled. Frankie, you can bring Nikki home after you guys are done here."

Frankie relented. "Okay." This was another reason he wanted Karen. She was so giving and understanding. He rose from his chair and walked her out, promising to set things straight. Karen wanted to set something else straight. She was leaving to keep the peace not to surrender what she hoped was a future with Frankie and their daughter. Instead of a simple kiss on the cheek, she stood on her tiptoes and gave Frankie a subtle kiss on the lips and whispered, in his ear, "See you later."

Frankie had to stand there a few minutes to collect himself as he watched her stroll away. That was the opening he needed to pursue more with Karen. First, he had to see why Shayla had flipped the script on him. When he arrived back to the table, Shayla and Dawn were back, and all the ladies seemed to be engrossed in conversation with Nikki. That's when Frankie caught the look of victory in Shayla's eyes. She was okay with Nikki, but she wanted no part of Karen. *Oh boy*, he thought, *and so it begins, women and their fickle minds.*

Camille's Apartment

Benjamin tossed the salad he made for himself and Camille while he listened on his mobile device to Kevin's recap of his trip to Atlanta, and the consequential fight he had with Paige. Benjamin hated to hear that the relationship being over hurt Kevin, but, in his opinion, it was the logical step. Of course, he could not voice that at the present moment, so he continued to prepare dinner and simply listen. A smiled crossed his face when Camille came out showered and looking refreshed in her white terry cloth boyshorts and tank. She was also on her mobile device, no doubt listening to Paige's version of the drama. Ben gave Camille a wink, and she blew a kiss his way and sat down at her eat-in kitchen table.

Camille was getting comfortable with the way Ben catered to her. He was so attentive. She just wanted to enjoy the moment with him, but best friend duty called. Camille could not believe Paige had been arrested for attacking Mrs. Michelson. But then, why did Mrs. Michelson have such a problem with Paige? She had never done anything to Camille's knowledge to warrant being spat on, literally. Camille said thank you to Ben as he sat her plate down, and Paige stopped mid-sentence.

"Camille, why didn't you tell me Ben was over there? I will talk to you later." Before Camille could object, *call ended* appeared on her phone's screen. Apparently, Ben had the same fate with his conversation as she had because he placed his mobile device on the table and said, "Shall we say grace?" That was another trait Camille adored about Benjamin, his commitment to his faith. They both had renewed their lives with Christ and had begun the journey of healing together for their bodies, minds, and souls. The last few months seemed like an eternity, and that is what gave Camille pause. It was all moving so fast, and she was so caught up in it. She feared it was too good, too fast, to last.

"Penny for your thoughts," Ben said bringing her back.

Camille chuckled and said, "Just thinking about how fast we have been moving, and if we should slow down."

Ben frowned, "Cam, I am not rushing you into anything am I?"

Camille knew she had started this dinner off wrong because of her fears. She had to make it right. "Of course you haven't, Benjamin. It is just . . . I have always been independent, with my dad being overseas. Now, after just a few months, I find myself not just wanting you to confirm every decision I make, I feel like I need your approval." Camille dropped her head and picked up her fork, digging into her salad, avoiding Ben's gaze.

"Camille, look at me," Ben said sternly. Camille lifted her brown eyes up to his with, what Ben thought was, the look of an adorable little girl. "Camille, when something is real it does not take forever to know. I dated Lauren for seven years and could not commit to her. Did I love her? Yes, I always will. However, I knew deep down it was not the real thing that would last for the rest of my life. One night, as tragic as it was, I felt it with you." He reached for hands, and she quickly gave them. "Cam, we can slow down if you want because you have to feel this too. I don't need any more proof that you are my missing rib. Camille James, I am willing to wait seven years plus seven more if that is what it takes for you to feel we are meant to be." He kissed the inside palm of both her hands and begin eating his food.

Camille sat there stunned in her seat. She could not move. Those words were felt in her soul. She only moved when Ben said, "Cam, sweetie, eat your dinner. We will work at your pace."

Camille ate her food. *What a man.* Although she was not ready to verbally admit it, she felt it too. She was Benjamin George Adams' missing rib. They continued their meal, discussing current events and their best friends' breakup. They both thought the breakup was for the best, but they both knew Kevin and Paige were not done yet. They vowed to one another not let their friends' mess of a relationship filter into their blossoming love.

Later that evening, when Benjamin had returned home, he received a text message from Camille that said *Goodnight Adam, from your Eve. I feel it too.* With that. he screamed thank you, Jesus, at the top of his lungs and did a Holy Dance in his home office. Then he settled down and texted back. *Goodnight, My Eve, I love you.*

Camille could not stop the tears as she read, *Goodnight, My Eve, I love you.* She asked the Lord to give her the strength and wisdom to be what He wanted her to be and to show her how to be what Ben needed her to be. She then texted back a happy face and *sweet dreams.*

Capriccio Grill, Peabody Hotel

Dawn and Autumn had taken Nikki to some of the downtown toy shops to start their spoiling of her right away. Shayla and Frankie were left at the table drinking coffee after their meal and dessert. Shayla began the conversation. "Nikki is a beautiful little girl, very intelligent for the rough start her life had. But she is cut from your cloth, and we will help her develop to be a young lady like Dawn and Autumn."

Frankie could not believe his ears. "What rough start are you speaking of, Shayla?" he asked with an attitude and raised eyebrows.

Shayla smiled and said, "Don't get upset. I just mean, clearly, her mother lacks judgment. You said yourself—you were not notified about the pregnancy and birth of Nikki because she did not know your complete legal name."

Frankie said firmly, "Shayla, I did not know hers either, and between Nikki's two parents, Karen is by far the most fit. My little girl is smart and not lacking in any area because of her mother. Karen made a mistake one night with me, but since then, she has *been every woman* to Nikki and herself."

"Frankie, please lower your voice. You barely know this girl. Yet, you parade her in here like she is some angel sent from above. Don't forget who has been there for you. Me and our girls have been to hell and back with you; not Miss One-night Stand."

Frankie sighed, "There it is."

"There what is?" Shayla asked firmly.

"You are jealous."

"What do I have to be jealous of, Frankie? Tell me."

"You, my dear Shayla, are jealous that I have found something with Karen. Yes, our first night together was less than ideal, but we made someone beautiful together. For the first time in our lives, you had nothing to do with something wonderful for me, and you can't handle it."

Shayla was shaken by his bluntness. Since being sober, Frankie had never had cross words with her. He always treated her with respect as his ex-wife and children's mother. If ever he didn't, it was because of drinking and, or, drugs. But this Frankie was stone sober, and their relationship was ending right before her eyes. Pure hatred swelled in her chest for Karen and Nikki. *How could he think of moving on?* No, she did not want to remarry him because of the Hell of his addiction, but she was not going to marry anyone else. Since his recovery, they were better than ever, sharing everything, being there for the girls. A couple of times they even made love, and that did not change the nature of their new friendship. How could Frankie move on with some tramp who got high and drunk and conceived a bastard child? Nikki was nothing more than a whining little crack head herself. No. She would not allow it, nor would she continue to sit here and let Frankie treat her this way. She began gathering her things as she spoke. "Frankie, you go ahead and play family with this little girl. When you find yourself lost, drunk and alone, just remember it was you who chose this." Shayla, with her purse under her arm, stood and stormed out of the restaurant. She had ridden in with her daughters, so she called a car service and left alone.

Frankie was amazed that Shayla would not want him to find happiness. Surely, she did not think their friendship with occasional benefits was healthy. Frankie paid the check and called Dawn to find out where they were with Nikki. He explained he and Shayla had words and told them he would drop by in a day or so to check on her. They were pleased with that and told him their mom just needed time.

Meanwhile, Nikki was elated to have every Shopkin from season one and two and all the accessories now. Uncle Ben had bought her some, but her big sisters finished the entire set. She could not have been happier. She jumped in her Daddy's arms and said, "I love you, and my sisters and my mommy. I am so happy." That brought tears to Frankie's and his two grown daughters' eyes. They walked to their cars, arms linked together. Frankie could not be a prouder dad.

Frankie carried his sleeping baby girl up the stairs in one arm, and her bags of toys in the other, while he climbed the stairs to Karen's apartment. He was definitely winded as he lifted the brass door knocker to alert Karen they were outside. Karen opened the door with a smile. Her beauty and smile took the rest of Frankie's breath away.

Karen, oblivious to Frankie's tiredness, took the bags from him and motioned with her hands for him to enter. She told him to follow her to put Nikki into her bed. Frankie did as she instructed. He could not get his brain to function enough to tell his mouth to say something, so he just followed like a puppy with his tongue hanging out. Upon entering Nikki's bedroom, he was overwhelmed with pride. Karen had given their little girl a room for a princess. Everywhere there was sugar and spice and everything nice. Her room had a beautiful pink canopy twin bed with a rail. Her walls were painted with a mural of the sun and clouds in the sky. She had a dry erase board mounted on her wall, where you could see Nikki's drawings and her practicing her name in script. There was a little grocery store set up, a kitchen, and play area where all things were Shopkin. Finally, he could speak.

"Karen, you have our baby girl's room so beautiful. Thank you for loving her when I was not around."

Karen blushed and waved him off. "Frankie, would you stop bringing up that you haven't been here stuff. You are here now, and that's what matters. Come on, let's take her shoes and socks off so that she can finish her nap."

Frankie did as he was instructed, and after Nikki was tucked in, he kissed her forehead. He followed Karen out, after she turned on Nikki's bed lamp, and closed her door.

Sitting on Karen's sofa, Frankie and she shared a glass of sweet tea and began a much-needed conversation. Frankie took the lead. "Karen, I want to apologize for Shayla's behavior today. She was out of line, and I told her as much."

Karen was happy he addressed Shayla but was hoping it was not in front of their daughters. "When did you address Shayla? I hope not in front of the twins and Nikki."

Frankie shook his head emphatically. "Of course not, the twins had taken Nikki shopping, and she should have all that Shopkins stuff now." He and Karen both chuckled at that. "Anyhow, when they left, I asked Shayla what her problem was, and can you believe she is jealous?" Karen looked at Frankie as if he had two heads. "Karen, why are you looking at me like that?"

"Frankie, surely you are not this clueless. Shayla is still in love with you. It was all over her face."

"I was clueless until she started ranting about how she can't believe I would move on."

Karen took Frankie's hand and looked him directly in the eyes.

"Frankie, are you ready to move on, can you?" He gave her a look of love and admiration.

"Karen, I can move on if you are ready to take this step with me." He said as he caressed her hands that were now in his and leaned in watching her to see if she would draw back. He did not have to wait long as Karen closed the gap, and they enjoyed their first kiss of passion without alcohol or drugs. It was one full of emotions and hope for a new beginning. Frankie was the first to pull away. "Karen, I like the way you just responded, but I prefer you answer my question verbally."

Karen swallowed and looked up at Frankie with her light brown eyes focused on his lips, then his eyes. "Yes, Frankie, I would like to move on with you, and see what we can become. You, me, and Nikki."

Frankie then pounced onto Karen with an aggressive kiss. It led to so much passion that again they were caught up in one another and moved to Karen's bedroom to begin their relationship with the act of making love.

ITS Transit Systems

Camille sipped her hot green tea as she listened to Karen recap her romantic night with Frankie. Karen spoke about Frankie as if he was truly her knight in shining armor. While Camille was happy that Nikki had her father and Karen seemed to have found love, she was not happy about the way Karen consented to sex without validating where the relationship was leading to. In fact, Camille, wondered if Karen had given any thought to their vows to stay celibate until marriage. All of this went through her mind as Camille tried not to show any judgmental expressions. She certainly understood how abstaining could be difficult because she had several thoughts about Ben in that manner. However, she resisted temptation by setting limitations with Ben's agreement on how far they could go physically. For starters, Benjamin does not enter her bedroom when he is visiting, nor do they sit in one another's arms while watching television or movies. They had tried that once, and the kissing and foreplay got out of hand, but they stopped themselves and made the pact not to go that route again. They pray every night together in person or over the phone. They have weekly bible study together at the kitchen table of one of their homes. The hardest thing for them to do was to leave one another's home by ten p.m. It was challenging to do that because they enjoyed each other's company, and time sped up when she was in his presence. Another great thing about their relationship was that they both were busy with their careers. Both Camille and Benjamin were normally exhausted by nine p.m., after dinner and their evening walk. Obviously, Karen and Frankie did not intend to set any boundaries. *So much for Karen keeping her temple holy.*

"Camille, did you hear me?" Karen exclaimed with a look that said her patience with Camille was wearing thin.

Camille, replaying Karen's last words quickly, tried to remember the question Karen asked. "I heard you, and no Benjamin and I have not been intimate yet. We don't plan to have sex unless we are married." Camille raised an eyebrow at Karen. "I also recall you being on the altar with me at Liberty Fellowship, vowing abstinence until marriage as well. Did you discuss that with Frankie before you two fell in bed together?"

Camille regretted sounding so motherly because Karen was, in fact, a grown woman. It just seemed she did not attempt to resist fornication and jumped in bed because Frankie told his ex-wife off and said he wanted to try with her. It was hard for Camille to believe he wasn't trying only to make a move on Karen.

"Camille, you are not seriously trying to tell me I am wrong for making love with the father of my child." Karen said this with attitude that was palpable. "If you are, I can promise I will not be sharing anything else with you. I am a grown woman, and I love Frankie, you cannot tell me this is wrong."

"Karen, I am not trying to tell you what you should or should not do or with whom you can do it with. However, I am asking you about the spiritual commitment you made to serve Christ and to avoid fornication. We learned in bible study together that we were cleansed from our sin by Jesus's blood, and we accepted him as our savior, and the Holy Spirit as our comforter. I want to know; did you give thought to that commitment that you made?"

"Camille, Frankie being the father of my child is a sign from Jesus Christ himself that he is who I need to be with. He is no longer the random dude I had a one-night stand with after getting drunk and high to deal with my pain and grief. Frankie made a commitment to me and Nikki that he will be there, like he has been since he found out about her. If giving him sexual gratification is what he needs, then I will be giving it to him. I also learned in Bible study that we should not judge and that God sees our hearts. Clearly, you don't practice everything taught in Bible study, *now do you, Camille!*"

Karen was now beyond angry, and her voice was elevated loud enough that Camille knew the other employees could hear them. "I can't believe I came in here thinking you would be happy for me, but no, Ms. Always Perfect and Right has something negative to say about poor Karen. Camille, you were there for me when I found out I was pregnant. You did not judge me when I told you the circumstances of Nikki's conception. You just loved me and helped me. Now, because I had passion with a man that could very well be my future husband, you stand there holier-than-thou, judging me. Well, guess what Camille, let's see how long Ben stays around while you play Ms. Chasity Belt."

Karen did not give Camille a chance to utter a word. She got up, said she had a meeting to get to, and slammed Camille's office door behind her.

Camille sat there amazed, but before she could gather her thoughts and process what had occurred with Karen, the receptionist buzzed in that Mr. J. D. James was in the lobby waiting to see her. Elated, Camille told her to send him up.

"Hey, Daddy, what a pleasant surprise," Camille said while rising to her feet to hug her dad.

"Hey, Camille, how is daddy's girl feeling?"

"Daddy, I am well, thanks for asking," Camille said as she rolled her eyes. She would forever be a twelve-year-old to her dad. She went back behind her desk to sit as J. D. took a seat flanking her desk. "So, what brings you by Daddy?"

J. D. cleared his throat and played with the cufflinks on his dress shirt. Camille watched him. *That is so unlike him. He normally looks eye to eye when in conversation.* Never had she seen him behave in this manner. "Daddy," she called out to get him to look at her.

"Tell me what's been bothering you, besides my accident."

J. D. looked up at his girl and said, "It is Karen. I believe I am her father."

Camille pushed back from her desk and walked around to sit next to her father in the matching chair beside him. "Daddy, what are you talking about?" Camille's voice cracked. Surely, she had misheard him.

"I need you to tell me if her mother's name is Cynthia Locke." Camille gasped and put her hand over her mouth. *Could this day get any worse?*

"Yes, Daddy, it is. How did you know her?"

J. D., filled with guilt, looked at his baby girl and said, "It's best I keep that to myself."

Bam, that was her answer. *Yes, this day could get worse.* She had just pissed off one of her best friends, and that best friend could be her half sister. "Wow!" Was all Camille could say or think at the moment.

Chapter 4: Confessions, Obsessions, and Progressions

"Let me make sure I have this correct, Daddy." Camille gave J. D. a puzzled look. "You are coming to me, asking Karen's mother's name and telling me she may be your daughter?"

"Yes," J. D. said firmly.

Camille waited for more, but that wait was in vain. She saw that she was going to have to drag each detail out of him for herself. "Daddy, you have to give me more than this. Karen is one of my best friends and not to mention my Executive Business Assistant. I am her daughter's godmother. Nikki calls me Tee-Tee, Now, by the little you have shared, I may be that . . . literally! Daddy, you are going to have to come clean, give me something to go on that's better than this!" Camille was losing her temper and knew she could not disrespect her father, but if he did not start sharing, she was going to lose it.

"Camille, calm down. You don't need to get worked up, okay." J. D. knew he was being sketchy with his delivery, but he simply did not know how to explain. But by the look on his baby's girl face, he was going to have to give details. He took Camille's hands and said, "Camille, remember when your mom was sick when you were young?" Camille nodded her head yes. "Well, I did the best I could, taking care of her and loving her until she succumbed to the breast cancer. When I lost Rachel . . . baby girl, I was so lost. When Grammy stayed with us that year after your mom's death, I had a fling with someone."

It was making sense to Camille now. She was seven years old when her mom died. At thirty-three, she had very few memories of her mom, but she knew that her parents were in love. She believed she knew where this conversation was headed but decided to remain silent and let her dad tell his story.

"Camille, I was so hurt and lonely. I started hanging out at a friend's bar, and this beautiful woman was singing a Diana Ross and the Supremes' song "Love is Here and Now You're Gone" . . ." J. D. looked down at the floor and shook his head as if trying to fight back all the demons of despair and grief. "Cynthia sang that song with such passion. Although Rachel had died and not simply walked away, it was true—I was that song. I had all this love with no one to give it to, and no one to return it."

Camille reached out and took her daddy's hand, giving it a gentle squeeze. J. D. smiled and squeezed her hand back and began again. "After Cynthia's set, we talked and shared drinks. To make a long story short, many nights after Grammy and I would put you down I met with Cynthia. She was only a temporary replacement for a void I have had since Rachel left this earth. After one look at Karen, I knew. She is the spitting image of Cynthia. Cynthia had some features that were similar to Rachel, and that was another draw I had to her. However, I was not interested in bringing a junkie around my little girl, so I just let her go. Camille, have you seen Cynthia?"

Camille looked at her father with sadness. "No, Daddy. Cynthia died when Karen was five or six from a stray bullet of a drive-by while leaving a club she was working at." This statement brought the tears, that J. D. was trying to fight off, streaming down. Never in a million years would he have thought Cynthia would be gone.

"Who took care of Karen?"

Camille sighed and said, "She was placed in her Aunt Esther's care, but the streets took care of her."

J. D. gasped and covered his face with both hands. Camille leaned in and took her daddy in her arms and rocked him with love and understanding. She would give him time to absorb what he may have turned his back on. Then they would be finding out if Karen was her sister.

Benjamin's Home Office

Benjamin set at his desk in his home office, listening to his team of engineers go over their caseloads for the day. Benjamin, as a senior vice president of a software storage firm, headed the Southeast region of the country. Benjamin's team consisted of over two-hundred field agents who worked in a joint effort to manage over three-thousand corporate accounts. The team ensured their client's servers and data were secure and up to date, according to federal regulations and ISO compliances. This was the region's afternoon call to recap the day's events and any unresolved issues. Ben only chimed in when asked direct questions that his managers, supervisors, or leads could not answer.

His thoughts drifted to Camille. She was the most beautiful woman he had ever encountered. She was everything he could have hoped and prayed for. Although she was educated and ran a successful business, there was an innocence and a naiveté about her. This made her have that submissive quality he wanted in a wife. As he thought about her beauty, he smiled because she had a simple and natural beauty, but she was always demure and elegant. She did not have to have designer labels, which made him want to shower her with every name brand he could buy. Her willpower to overcome the physical challenges she had, due to the accident, made her a case study. Camille had a positive outlook on life, and that had her back in the office six weeks earlier than the doctors had predicted. Ben had expected that, by now, he would have, at least, one complaint about Camille. Something that would give him pause, but there was no wrong he could find in her. *Camille James is perfect.* What made it better was that she got along with his mom. What a dream come true. His girl and mother took to one another immediately. His mother had given him her seal of approval on Camille. Ben was shocked when Camille first said she and his mom frequently talked, about any- and everything including scriptures. Ben smiled knowing he had found the one. He was planning on proposing to her at the family get together that was coming up.

"Mr. Adams, are you there, sir?" Mark, one of his leads, snapped Ben's attention back to the call. Ben had to think for a moment about the issue the team was discussing, and then he responded adamantly. "Yes, it is imperative and mandatory that all cases are closed in the unit database within two hours of leaving the client's site. This can be done in your company-provided cars before leaving the premises, as each engineer and field agent has a mobile hot spot, mobile device, laptop, and tablet. There is no reason for any employee to be in the red with compliance in closing cases. Understood?"

After the call had wrapped up with yes sirs and no problems, Ben took his personal mobile device out and scrolled down his contacts to Cam's picture. He needed to hear her voice. However, before he could make the call, his doorbell rang. Benjamin opened the door to a distressed looking Kevin. "Kevin, what's up man? Come on in. You look like something is on your mind."

Kevin walked in and proceeded to Ben's living room, flopping down on the brown leather sofa. Kevin sighed and rubbed his hand across his head, and then his face. Ben, sitting across from Kevin in a brown leather La-Z-Boy chair, bent forward to get a closer look at Kevin.

"Man, what is going on, something else happened with Paige, or work?"

Kevin looked at Benjamin with defeat written all over his face. "Ben, man, it's all of the above. This entire day, week, and month has been a struggle. I told you about the fight Paige and I had. That is on my mind and my heart, man. Today—when I got back in the office after being gone for three days because I have a momma and girl that behave like they are starring in a reality TV show—my voice mail had twenty-five messages, my email was full, and I had to present to the grand jury today. To make matters worse, not one of my witnesses showed up, and the defense attorney had a field day serving my behind to me. Meanwhile, my mom is calling me nonstop, ranting about Paige, and that she may need plastic surgery. What can I do? I apologized, man. She is my mom, and my girl literally beat her behind!" Ben took that "my girl" reference and jumped in.

"So, you and Paige back together?"

Kevin gave Ben an incredulous look. "No, I haven't talked to Paige since she stormed out a couple of days ago. But I am not going to lie. I miss her like mad."

Ben was thrown by the statement. If anyone ever physically assaulted his mom, no matter what reason they had, there would be no more thoughts of them, not to mention missing her. However, Ben knew Kevin had it bad for Paige, so he just listened.

"Ben, I know I should just be done with her. I have so much on my plate, not to mention I am still trying to find the fool who hit Camille. I am just not ready to walk away from Paige. I'm just giving her time to cool down."

Ben was not shocked by that declaration, but he had to ask a question. "Kevin, I cannot tell you what to do or how to feel, but I need you to explain why you can't live without Paige?"

Kevin looked up at Ben with a smirk. "Aww, man . . . that girl is unpredictable and buck wild. But she is loyal and has pride in everything she does. I don't know why my mom pushes her buttons, and Paige lets her, but if that were not the case, we would be a match made in heaven."

"Are you sure that's it?"

Kevin flashed all thirty-two of his pearly whites. "Paige being buck wild is an understatement for Paige in the bedroom. That girl does things to me that brings me to my knees. There is no way I can live without her."

"Is it worth your mom getting hurt, and Paige serving time?"

Kevin said with his hands up. "Of course not, I just don't know what to do. Maybe I need to go to church with you and Camille."

Ben put his hands on Kevin's shoulder while speaking to him. "We would love to have you at church, and you my friend, have a problem only Jesus can handle. Come on let's grab some sodas and catch the game."

Kevin looked confused. "Soda? Jesus, man, what is Camille doing to have you drinking soda? You don't have any kind alcohol or something? Dawg, I need a real drink!"

Ben shrugged and said, "No, Camille and I are on bent knees in prayer together, my friend, trying to do it the good book's way."

Karen's apartment

Karen did not make it past her couch after she left work early. In need of time to sort through her thoughts, Karen did not even pick up Nikki from daycare. She laid on her couch crying. She could not believe the blow up she just had with Camille. Camille was like family to her and Nikki. Karen could not understand why sleeping with someone she already had a child with and planned to be with forever was wrong. Didn't a commitment count? Why should she miss out on love? Frankie only wanted the best for her and their family. He stood up for her to his ex-wife, an ex-wife that he admitted was his best friend. Would he have done that if their love was not real? Karen was a wreck going back and forth in her mind about the commitment she made to Christ, and the future she wanted with Frankie. Would Frankie end things if she did not continue a sexual relationship with him?

Karen thought about the singles ministry Bible Study, where Pastor Caine gave the singles the scripture, 1 Corinthians 6:18-20. He explained how Christian singles were to resist committing sin with their body. She remembered how she looked at her body when she got home after hearing that it was a temple for the Holy Spirit that dwelled inside of her. With tears streaming down, she got up and read the entire passage out loud.

"Flee fornication, every sin that a man doeth is without the body; but he that committed fornication sinneth against his own body." Karen's sobs were now audible. She threw the bible across the room. It was better not to know this. Now she had to be honest with herself, she wanted to slap Camille for being right. What she did with Frankie, and every man she had ever been sexually intimate with, was wrong.

Karen continued to wail as if a death had occurred. She had a problem. How could she have it all—the Man and Peace with the Lord? Karen continued to weep as her wails turned to deep moans of agony. Her stomach cramped and her head ached because her spirit was willing, but her flesh was weak. Her sobs lasted for what seemed like hours. She was sinking deep into despair when the doorbell rang. She slowly dragged her aching body off of the couch. On the way to the door, she glanced at her reflection in the wall mirror, her eyes were red and swollen. Karen just shook her head trying to snap out of the pity party she was throwing herself. When she opened the door, there Frankie stood with flowers in one hand and toys in the other. The tears she was trying to hold back burst out as if a levee to her heart had broken.

Frankie hurriedly nudged her into her apartment, sat down the flowers and toys, and grabbed Karen to him.

"What is wrong, sweetie? What has happened, is Nikki okay?" Frankie asked while holding Karen around the waist and rubbing her hair as her head rested on his chest. Karen with sobs and hiccups tried to tell him, but nothing she said made sense. He led her to the couch and positioned her on his lap and said, "Karen, I can't help, honey, if you don't calm down and tell me what is wrong. Come on, baby girl, tell me the problem."

Karen took deep breaths and tried again. This time her words came out audibly. "I've messed up with you, Frankie. I should be setting a good Christian example for Nikki, but I did not think twice before sleeping with you. I made a commitment to honor Christ and be holy, but when you told me we could try, I let all my newfound standards and vows go." Karen wiped away the tears that were now falling again and continued. "I want to be a good woman, Frankie. No more self-sabotaging only to have to spend months and years repairing the damage I've done to myself. But, I am not prepared to lose you before we get started, I just can't."

Karen fell back on the couch and shielded her face with her arm. She began to cry again. She knew she looked a mess in front of Frankie. Snot was running from her nose, but she could not stop crying.

Frankie was at a loss. He thought their being intimate was a good thing. However, Karen was crying as if she committed murder. Frankie knew the importance of acknowledging a higher power for strength; he called on God frequently as a recovering alcoholic. He never thought that something as wonderful as lovemaking could cause Karen or anyone to feel so much guilt. He went to God through prayer in Jesus's name for his sobriety and his family's well-being. By all accounts, he considered himself a Christian. Was she implying he was not? He needed to ask Karen questions because she was obviously leading to something he may consider a deal breaker for their relationship. Looking at her now, he knew she was not up for questions. All he could do at this time was to console a sobbing Karen. He wondered if he would lose her to this guilt. After an hour, Karen was asleep tucked in her bed. She had cried for so long that her body was shivering while she slept. Frankie knew it was time for Nikki to be picked up. He decided to let Karen rest, and he went to get their daughter.

Frankie beamed with pride as he scooped up Nikki in his arms. He rarely picked up Dawn and Autumn from daycare when they were this age because Shayla did that. But having his baby girl lead him around to introduce him to her teachers and friends at the daycare was a memory he would cherish forever. When he had her locked in the car seat, he left Karen a message that Nikki would be with him for the next few hours and not to worry. He was headed straight to Benjamin's for some advice. Maybe he or Camille could give him a clue on how to help Karen. Hopefully, in the process, he could save his new family.

****

It was like the 1980's movie, *Three Men and a Little Lady*. Nikki had Frankie, Benjamin, and Kevin strung out after a few hours. She had them playing tea party, watching episodes of Shopkins, and finally she "let it go," while they watched *Frozen*. She fell asleep before the movie was twenty minutes in. All three men were worn out and grateful that the three-year-old had succumbed to siesta.

Frankie cleared her leftover chicken nugget kid's meal off her cartoon dinner tray. Uncle Benjamin had purchased the dinner tray the last time she and Camille were over. Frankie was grateful for the bond Karen and Nikki had with family and friends. They all were fast becoming his family as well, which led him to join Ben and Kevin in the game room. The room was definitely a man cave. It had a one-hundred-inch flat-screen television mounted to the wall with a digital surround sound system. The furniture was oversized brown leather sofas and La-Z-Boy chairs. There was a pool table, three different gaming systems, and a bar that did not appear to be stocked with alcohol, for which Frankie was grateful. There were energy drinks and bottled water instead. The men sat at the high top table talking as if they were having a meeting of knights at the round table. As soon as Frankie sat down, Benjamin got to the point.

"So, Frankie, I am sure you did not just come over to let Kevin and I know what babysitting felt like. How are things going with you and Karen?"

Frankie dropped his head and said, "Man, I came for advice. Karen and I moved our relationship to the next level a couple of days ago. It was magic. I never felt anything like what we shared before, even after being married to Shayla for years. So today, when I got off work, I rushed over to her apartment with flowers in hand for Karen and toys for my baby girl. I was thinking I was going to recreate the magic before we had to pick up Nikki. But what I got was a sobbing Karen. It was like she had committed murder, or her best friend had died. I tried to console her, so I could figure out what was wrong. But she only babbled stuff about her letting Jesus down and not keeping her vows and commitment."

Frankie ran his hand across his head and dropped his forehead on his arms as he folded them on the table. Ben reached over and patted him on the back.

"My friend, you are dealing with a woman of Christ who feels guilty for backsliding."

Frankie lifted his head. "Backsliding from what?" Frankie was so confused, and Benjamin could see it all over his face. Kevin looked on because he was just as lost on how to respond to Karen's reaction.

Benjamin raised his hands in surrender. "I understand how you could be confused if you did not grow up in the church. Fortunately for you, I did. See, when a woman has committed her life to Christ and become saved, she can no longer commit sin. One of those sins is fornication or sex outside of marriage."

Frankie was puzzled. "What? Why? Because she is a sex addict she has to abstain, like I am a recovering alcoholic, so I can't take a drink."

Benjamin shook his head. "No, it's not that she is a sex addict. She has accepted that her body is the temple of the Lord and has to be free from sexual sin until she is married."

Frankie was not believing his ears. "Ben, I attend church almost every Sunday. I haven't heard I can't have sex if I am in a committed relationship. But then, I really don't know what Shayla's pastor is whooping and hollering about half of the time. I know that I go to God as my source. He is my higher power to help me with my sobriety. So, you mean to tell me, Karen is not a Christian if she makes love to me? That she is going to Hell because we are not married?"

Benjamin could see the rise in Frankie's temperature, and he understood. He had been there with Lauren and all the other women he dated until Camille. He would let them know he was not ready for marriage and was not practicing celibacy. However, with Camille, he was honoring their vows to the Lord and honoring her body as the temple of God it was. It was hard to hold out because Camille's body looked like it was the truth. He thought for a few minutes on what to say to Frankie, knowing that he who won a soul was wise. It was not lost on him that Kevin, a non-believer, was in their company as well. Kevin and Paige definitely needed Jesus in their relationship.

"Frankie, the best thing I can tell you is to talk to Karen. It's great you have given her this time to get a cooler head, but you must talk this out. Then I advise you to attend a Bible class at our church for dating while saved. It is called 'Don't stir Up or Awaken Love Until it Pleases.' It covers why Christians should abstain from sex and gives great direction on how to avoid getting caught up. It has been a blessing for me and Camille. I am not telling you it is easy to abstain, but this class will give you the Biblical reference to show why it is the Lord's will. If Karen is worth it, you will attend the class with her and wait until she is ready."

Frankie had a look of bewilderment. "Has Karen been attending this class, Ben?"

"Yes, she has been there every time I've made it with Camille. Just come, and you will see why she feels the guilt she does." Ben looked to his friend Kevin with a lopsided smirk. "Yo, Kev, it would not hurt you and Paige to attend either. Because one of you might be doing time if this thing with her and your mother is not settled."

Kevin raised an eyebrow. "Really now, Pastor Ben? You have been celibate for what, three of four months? This is after years of whoredom. Okay, I will take it into consideration. I will see if I can fit that into my schedule. Although, I am up to my neck with paperwork and still coming up empty on the driver of the Expedition that hit your Holy Woman." Frankie and Kevin laughed out loud at that comment.

Ben just gave them both a nod in acceptance and said, "Hey, make all the jokes you want. I have found my soul mate, and we are proceeding along nicely to a happily ever after. So you clowns take all the jabs you want. I can guarantee you I won't have years of celibacy. I am ready to put a ring on it."

Kevin put up a stop signal with his hand. "Dude, calm down, I hear you I am just serious, I mean joking." They all laughed, and then a thought occurred to Frankie.

"Kevin, I've been meaning to talk to you about something a friend of mine let me in on that may help the hit-and-run case," Frankie said. Both Ben and Kevin ceased all movements.

Kevin turned one hundred percent into a prosecuting attorney. "What information do you have, and why haven't I heard of it before now?"

"I am sorry, Kevin. I was waiting until you were in your office when I dropped off the mail, but you been MIA."

Ben, frustrated with the small talk, jumped in. "Frankie, tell us what you know."

"Okay, I ran into one of the guys I had dinner with the same day you all said Camille was hit. It was in the afternoon, a pre-bachelor party so to speak. Well, I found out the wedding didn't happen because the groom got drunk and hit something, he could not remember what. He had gone to an ex's house, where he was found the next day when he should have been at the wedding. Long story short, it struck a nerve, being the same date and all. So, I asked what type of car he drove, and it is indeed a Ford Expedition." Benjamin did not know whether to hug or strangle Frankie, but he kept his composure because they now had a lead.

Kevin asked the name of the driver. Frankie gave him Brian Andrews' information, including his home address. Kevin took the information and left to do some investigating with his staff.

Frankie parted ways soon after as Nikki woke up, saying she wanted to go home to her mommy. He wanted to go home to her mommy too, to settle this backsliding issue. He was determined to make this work, and if going to this Bible class would keep him from seeing Karen that way again, then that was what they were going to do.

Camille's Apartment

Camille sat in her bedroom on the edge of her bed in a white terry cloth robe after a hot shower. The last week had revealed so much in her life and circle of friends. She had yet to speak with Karen about them being half sisters. Karen had called in sick the remainder of the week after their fight. She had not answered any of Camille's phone calls over the weekend. Then there was her dad who was set on just leaving things as they were and actually left the country saying she was in good hands with Benjamin and her friends. He had received a call from his superior's overseas. There was an urgent matter only he could handle. Camille did not believe that for one minute. Camille knew it was wrong, but she wanted to slap her dad and tell him a thing or two. If she could have just called him the biggest coward to his face, it would have subsided some of the turmoil she felt inside. How could he be a wonderful father to her and not so much as want to acknowledge he helped create Karen and had a granddaughter?

In the next instant, Camille's mind migrated to Paige who was in her spare bedroom. Camille had spent Friday and Saturday consoling Paige. Although Paige informed her that she left Kevin's place with vigor and her dignity intact, Camille wanted to know where it was lost between his house and hers. Paige had been a babbling, crying love fool all weekend. Thinking of love snapped her mind to Benjamin, her president and leader of her heart. The heart that was racing as she thought about him. She had not seen him this weekend because of dealing with her dad and Paige. She missed him fiercely. She closed her eyes and deeply inhaled thinking about all the kindness and love he bestowed upon her. She shook her head at the sudden nervousness that came over her as she thought about meeting his extended family after church later today. She felt good knowing Mother Ellen was on her side. Mother Ellen was a powerful woman of God that Camille was grateful to have in her life. She could not wait to get to church. Surely, Mother Ellen would help Camille with her half sister crisis and maybe even help with Paige. Paige was joining her at Liberty this morning. She knew Kevin was going to come with Benjamin too. Camille got up off the bed to dress for church, and silently, she said, "Father God, please heal, deliver, and set free today in your sanctuary. We all need your power, In Jesus Name, Amen."

Chapter 5: Exchanges

Liberty Fellowship Church

Liberty Fellowship Church was a medium-sized church with a congregation of 1200 to 1500 members who attended the two Sunday morning worship services. Camille had become a member after falling in love with Mother Ellen who taught her Women's Sunday School class, and the teaching style of Pastor Derrick Caine. Pastor D, as he was passionately called by the congregation, was in his mid-forties and approached the Gospel of Christ with authority while making sure his members could apply the word practically to their life. The church was non-denominational. Pastor D had stated in the 'First Things First Class' Camille attended that he wanted a church that embraced all cultures and promoted kingdom building by meeting the natural and spiritual needs of all members. With all the outreach ministries the church had, Liberty was accomplishing that goal. The church offered free counseling provided by licensed therapists who were Christians, food pantries and shelters for those exiting prison, domestic abuse counseling, foreign language classes, and so much more.

Camille was supposed to start volunteering in the Children's ministry with Karen. Now that was up in the air because she had upset Karen by being judgmental. Camille regretted their fight, and not just because Karen could be her sister, but because she should have just prayed about the situation and kept her mouth closed.

Camille was snapped out of her thoughts when the Pastor's wife, Emily, came and gave her a sincere hug and told her how wonderful she looked. She also told her she could see God's physical healing was almost one hundred percent. Camille believed her because all of her scars were gone. Her hair was even on both sides now, and she loved it being shoulder length. Through physical therapy, the limp she had was gone, and there were no signs of any brain damage on her last scan. She had been truly healed by the Lord's stripes. Camille was blessed and thankful. Camille could feel the love and sincerity radiate from First Lady Emily. She was a pure soul, and after Camille had heard her testimony in the First Things First class, she was a kindred spirit with Camille. After the two stopped embracing, they both turned to see Benjamin dressed in an expensive, Italian, navy blue suit and imported shoes.

"First Lady Em." Benjamin smiled using the nickname he'd given her. "How are you doing today?"

"Hi, I am well, Brother Benjamin. You are looking handsome on this fine Lord's Day." Camille saw a twinkle in Lady Emily's eyes as they bounced between her and Benjamin.

Benjamin thanked her for the compliment and offered his own to her, with a brotherly hug. They said their goodbyes to Lady Emily and walked into the sanctuary together as she moved on to speak to more of the members and visitors. Camille and Benjamin normally sat together in the middle section of the sanctuary with his mother. It was the best seating to them both because they could clearly see the monitors, and the speakers were just the right volume midway.

Camille liked that the traditional praise and worship songs were delivered by an anointed praise and worship team. The lighting crew was awesome, knowing how to usher in the presence of the Lord with dimming the lights at the right moments. Some people felt it was too much of a production, but Camille enjoyed all the effort put into making sure the congregation got into the realm of true praise and worship. It was more effective to her than having praise and worship leaders ranting for the congregation to join in with them. Some churches did that because they did not understand how to lead people into worship. Rather, they wanted the people coming for a refreshing and to cheer the praise team on instead of bowing at the Lord's feet in praise and worship. Camille came to understand the difference during a Bible study taught by the Women's Ministry Director. As the Praise and Worship team sang the beautiful, and time appropriate, song of Crystal Lewis "Beauty for Ashes," Camille stood to her feet and let her troubles go. The praise ministry delivered words of deliverance through song, and she thought of her family and circle of friends and said a silent prayer for them all.

Benjamin, who was to Camille's left, was on his feet engaged in the worship until he opened his eyes and saw the two couples taking their seats in front of him. It was Frankie and Karen along with Paige and Kevin. Although Frankie and Karen sat in between Kevin and Paige, they were all there. He thought how befitting a song it was for them to experience this morning. He closed his eyes and lost himself in honoring the creator who gave them unmerited favor, grace, and mercy.

He gives beauty for ashes
Strength for fear
Gladness for mourning
Peace for despair

After the praise and worship, Camille opened her eyes and was shocked to see their friends in front of her. Paige looked over her shoulder and winked. Karen did not move. Were those tears streaming down Frankie's face? Camille could not be sure. Camille may not have been sure about Frankie, but she was positive his girl was crying.

Frankie reached into his suit pocket and gave Karen his handkerchief. His hands were shaking as he gave it to her. He was praying this would not be a repeat of last week. Karen took it and wept into it. Frankie was at a loss, but he was willing to do anything he could to assist Karen in her Christian walk. After all, she was miserable, and her being right with Jesus could make her happy. He was ready to see her smile again. As he gently rubbed Karen on the back, he took in Liberty's atmosphere. It held a sense of peace while praise and worship were going on. He was excited to think this sanctuary indeed had a different spirit about it. He was hooked into the service and wanted to experience all of it.

Paige sat stoically and thought. Jesus had a lot of ashes to turn into beauty if her relationship was going to work. As far as she was concerned, she should just sweep those ashes right out the back door. *Humph.*

Kevin, who was raised Catholic, had no clue what to do during the service. No affirmations were read, and there were no hymnals. *Oh boy.* It was way out of his comfort zone.

The flow of the service followed its normal pattern; there were songs by the choir, offering, benevolence prayers for the sick, and then it was time for the Word of God.

Pastor Derrick Cain stepped up to the speaker's stand that his aide had placed up on stage. It was removable as the church had dramas and dances that a stationary pulpit would hinder. He was dressed in a black robe with red trimming and gold buttons that went up to his collar. He always welcomed the visitors and thanked his members for coming home. He acknowledged the love of his life, First Lady Emily, and his adult children, and the clergy on his roster. Then he got into the delivery of his message. Camille and Ben, alike, enjoyed the way Pastor D. did not move from his podium. There was no running around, whooping, or tuning up to sing his point across. He simply brought them the word of God. Today was no different.

Pastor Derrick Cain's Sermon

"Saints of God, today's message will be from the Book of Isaiah Chapter 61 verses 1-3.

"Let's stand and read it together from the King James Version. For those who do not have Bibles, the verses will display on monitors on both sides of the sanctuary.

"61, The Spirit of the Lord GOD is upon me; because the LORD hath anointed me to preach good tidings unto the meek; he hath sent me to bind up the brokenhearted, to proclaim liberty to the captives, and the opening of the prison to them that are bound;

"2, To proclaim the acceptable year of the LORD, and the day of vengeance of our God; to comfort all that mourn;

"3, To appoint unto them that mourn in Zion, to give unto them beauty for ashes, the oil of joy for mourning, the garment of praise for the spirit of heaviness; that they might be called trees of righteousness, the planting of the LORD, that he might be glorified.

"I first have to give thanks to our wonderful praise and worship team for breaking up the fallow ground with their ministry of songs. Their song has planted the seed for today's word. I am here to add the fertilizer, and the Spirit of God will add the rain and increase. Now, Verse 1, has resonated with your servant. I accepted my call to be minister of the gospel of twenty years ago. Fifteen years ago, I became the founding pastor of Liberty Fellow. It is a fact that this passage, the Spirit unction me share today is where the name of our ministry was birthed from. Before we delve deeper into the text, I want you know the whole purpose of Jesus Christ coming to earth in the flesh was to set us free. It's not complicated. He left glory, became flesh, walked this earth in human form to die for sin that had the world bound, what a man huh? The prophet Isaiah is a front of runner of the Messiah Christ. Many of Isiah's prophecies were manifested during Jesus' life. So today, I want you to be of good cheer. I come to you like Isaiah came to the people of Israel with good news. Now my good news is for a particular set of people, like some of the secular pop stars may say, 'This isn't for everybody,' but is open for all who choose to believe. To determine if you are in the group, this good news going out to is going to take self-reflection on your part. Only you and the Master above knows your heart and innermost thoughts. So, let's keep it real with ourselves today, shall we? The Good News today is: to the person who are down in their spirit (the meek), to the person who has a broken heart from a severed relationship, be it romantic or familial, to the person that is held captive in the prison of their mind, sin, or shame. If you are one of these people, no matter what has you bound, whether it is sexual sin, lies, stealing, drugs or alcohol abuse—don't worry you are in good company today, because so were some of us. Before I accepted Jesus Christ, I felt I was in a couple of those bondages. But today, the Good News is Jesus' blood that was shed and the fact that he was resurrected from the grave, gives us all the power to do a gift exchange. Now this exchange is not like the dirty Santa families play with one another, it's not like the secret Santa. The Lord wants your dirty gifts to exchange with his beautiful ones. Our text tells you he wants your ashes, whatever you think you have messed us so badly that it can't be fixed. Maybe your relationship is in ungodly state, give it to Him and he will exchange it for something beautiful and Holy meet me at the cross on the altar. If you are grieving in despair over the death of a loved one, divorce, or loss of job, exchange it with Jesus and He will give you a garment of praise. Whatever has you bound and imprisoned in your mind, hurt, pain, maybe a bad temper—exchange it with Jesus and get joy, hope, and peace instead of despair. Please stand, my message is done. It does not take long to give the good news of Jesus who wants to make a strength exchange today. Elders and Mothers meet these souls at the cross in prayer and for repentance. Praise Team lets have that song again. Oh, I feel the anointing! There is about to be exchanges in Jesus name."

As the praise team started to minister through song, the aisles of the church became filled with people who were ready for the strength exchange. Karen Locke was one of those people. She squeezed out of the aisle past Frankie without a thought of him. She was serious this time. She would not be going back to that place of barely hanging on for a trigger from her past, allowing herself to sink deeper into sin. Although she did not understand it fully, she admitted she was a person in bondage to sin, wrath, unforgiving of herself, and self-abhorring. She wanted to exchange it all at the altar.

Camille was behind Karen. She wanted to be there to say she was sorry and ask for forgiveness of her best friend. She also needed to exchange fear for strength. She had to tell Karen, who was already broken from rejection and abuse, that she had a sister and a coward for a father.

Benjamin saw that Frankie was struggling with the events of the service. He knew that Frankie attended church, but obviously it was not Pentecostal. Benjamin went up a row and asked, "You alright, man?"

"I want whatever this peace is," Frankie answered.

Benjamin pulled Frankie into a man hug. "There is room on the altar for you."

As Frankie made his way out of the aisle, he motioned to Kevin asking if he was ok. Kevin put on the politician smile and said, "I will wait here with Paige."

Like Hell, she would be waiting with him. Paige, out of sheer stubbornness, threw her head back with a scowl and rushed out of the aisle.

Ben smirked, *whatever gets her to the altar.*

Kevin took a seat with his face in his hands. The last forty-five minutes had simply been too much.

When Camille arrived at the altar, she was delighted Mother Ellen was with Karen. The two ladies were hugging. Tears streamed down Karen's face. Mother Ellen was praying for Karen while rubbing her back. Camille made her way over to them just to be close to Karen. Mother Ellen saw her first and said, "Here is your best friend." Karen turned around and saw Camille.

The two women said I'm sorry at the same time and then embraced. Mother Ellen smiled and moved to the next soul on the altar. Frankie and Benjamin were with Elder Samuel Carmichael in a prayer room. It was where people were taken who are new to the church or the Pentecostal way. It was a place for questions to be asked and answered. Frankie had asked how he could be saved and now understood—"That if you confess with your mouth to the Lord Jesus and believe in your heart that God has raised Him from the dead, you will be saved (Romans 10:9). Jesus answered and said to him, 'Most assuredly, I say to you, unless one is born again, he cannot see the kingdom of God'" (John 3:3).

Frankie accepted Jesus Christ as Lord in his life and savior of his soul. His new brother in Christ, Benjamin, was standing with him.

Paige stood on the altar with her hands up, wondering why did she just not go to the restroom. *Where was Mother Ellen?* Camille was always bragging on how gentle of a lady she was. Unlike this fool who was speaking in tongues in her ear, and her spittle was hitting the side of her face. Paige was about to snap, but she counted back from twenty. She needed to remain calm because this church meant a lot to Camille. Slapping this babbling old lady, who had now just stepped on her toes and her peep toe red bottoms, would not be a good look for her. Paige understood the message, and how to give her life to Christ. She didn't want to. Therefore, she closed her eyes and just said, "Thank you, Jesus!" That seemed to give this desperate church mother some form of victory, and she moved back and started doing a holy dance as if she just scored a touchdown.

Paige was willing to say and do whatever the mother wanted just to get rid of her. Paige confessed Jesus was Lord with her mouth, but not in her heart. Her heart was filled with too much bitterness and anger. She needed her walls up because there were too many Julia Michelsons and other people who wanted to kick you down in the world. Paige had to keep her guards up. Camille was the only friend with whom she had ever let them down.

After church dismissed, Paige made a mad dash to her car without saying a word to anyone. She had to get away from Liberty Fellowship. She wanted desperately to stop at the first bar and have a drink. She cried as she spoke aloud to herself. "Dealing with church folks makes a girl need a drink."

Paige was not against religion. She believed in Jesus Christ. He just was not into her life. When she was younger, and living with her Aunt Jane, there was a missionary that belonged to a sanctified church that would pick up all the kids and take them to Sunday school and worship service. She enjoyed going to Sunday school and started to pray that God would send her someone who would love her. Someone like her dad, whom she still had not met to this day, but back then she believed her prayers would cause him to look for her. When he found her, he would take her away from the projects, but that never happened. Instead, she was neglected by her aunt who only supplied her with the bare minimum of clothes and foods. To add insult to injury, Aunt Jane only helped her become pretty when the social workers would visit. Paige put in the prayer box that she wanted to be loved. She wanted to be wanted. She started to speak it aloud in her bedroom. Aunt Jane heard her praying and beat her with an extension cord until she bled. *Nope, Jesus did not answer that prayer either.* On reflection, by the age of fifteen and with no rescue in sight, she told herself she was the only person she could trust. If Jesus was her savior, why did he give her a drug addict for a mother? No, Jesus was not into her. However, she knew about self-empowerment. That is what she drew on when she was eighteen, and Aunt Jane kicked her out. She worked three jobs and put herself through school. The only miracle in her life that had not crumbled was her friendship with Camille. Paige blinked out of those tragic thoughts as she drove and wiped the tears from her eyes. She wanted a drink desperately and to go home and dive into her bed. But she could not do that. She had to go to the Adams' house. Benjamin was adamant, and she did not want to miss this dinner. There was nothing she would not do for Camille. She was grateful to God for sparing Mille's life. It was a good thing Ben and his mom were praying; otherwise, Camille would be in Heaven. Especially, if it were left up to Paige's prayers to be granted. Paige turned on one of her favorite pick me up songs by Mary J Blige, "Just Fine." She started to feel better as Mary belted out the girl-power lyrics.

Can't let this thing called love get away from you. Feel free right now, go do what you want to do, Can't let nobody take it away, from you, from me, from we-No time for moping around. Are you kidding? And no time for negative vibes, cause I'm winning.

Paige was coming around to herself. That was what she did. She looked into herself and found the strength to carry on that was all the exchange she needed. Paige made the right turn onto Mother Ellen's street and prepared herself to be a supportive friend. Whatever Ben had planned; it better be good.

****

Mother Ellen Louise Adams was a perfect southern host. She had taken her church suit and hat off and was now wearing a beautiful gold caftan. She looked like a walking angel to Benjamin who greeted her with a hug and kiss. As Camille stood by Ben's side, she could see the love Mother Ellen had for her only son. It was beautiful. Camille hoped if she ever had children they would be able to feel the love and warmth from her in the same manner. Mother Ellen let go of Benjamin and pulled Camille in for a hug. "Daughter, let's get you comfortable and out of these stuffy church clothes. I have something you can relax in. I also bought you one of those La-Z-Boy chairs Ben said was good on your body."

Camille blushed. "Mother Ellen, you did not have to do that."

"Nonsense, child, you are Ben's angel. We got to make sure you are all fixed up."

"Well, I certainly hope we have not forgot about Benjamin's true angel!"

Camille looked around to see who could have been responsible for that awful jab to her gut. She gasped as she recognized Mrs. Carol, Lauren's mother. She had met her at church, and the lady always seemed pleasant. She sat on their row by Mother Ellen on most Sundays. Camille was frozen in shock. She could not even take a glance at Ben who had pulled her firmly into his side.

Mrs. Carol was about five-feet-eight-inches tall. She had on a black two-piece suit, black opaque tights, and black ballerina flats. Her hair was in a basic bob without any sheen. She had ebony skin and wore no make-up. Her eyes were filled with grief, despair, and contempt. If there was a hole in the floor that could swallow Camille, she would have had no objections in disappearing at that moment.

Mother Ellen spoke with a controlled voice. "Carol, you know Camille, Benjamin's girlfriend. I told you she would be in attendance today, and hopefully, here on out. Daughter, this is Carol, a close family friend. I am sure Ben has informed you that she is the mother of our late beloved Lauren."

Camille was in love with Mother Ellen's compassion and ability to control the situation. It helped Camille relax. She extended her hand and said, "It is wonderful to meet you officially, Mrs. Carol. Benjamin has spoken of you and your husband in the highest regard. I'm sorry for your loss and hope to get to know you." Camille thought she did a great job. She did not make mention that she had spoken to this lady at church for the last six weeks, with no reply from her.

Mrs. Carol simply shook Camille's hand and walked off with what sounded like *humph*, but Camille could have been mistaken. She had finally taken a glance at Benjamin, and the only description that could match the look on his face was that of a scowl. Benjamin asked his mom, without turning to look at her, his gaze was fixed on Mrs. Carol's back exiting the room, "Mom, why did you invite her?"

"Ben, she comes over to all the big Sunday dinners. She has for the last nine years."

Benjamin ground his teeth. He did not count on having to deal with Lauren's mother. He shook it off and turned to look eye to eye with Camille while rubbing the outside of both her arms. "Are you okay, Cam? We can leave if you want to."

Camille gave him a look of disgust. "No way, Benjamin Adams. I want to meet your extended family. I understand Mrs. Carol is still grieving. You can replace a girlfriend or lover, but she can't replace her only daughter. It has to be difficult for her to see me . . . us. She will have to accept it, so no running away." She pulled her arms out of Ben's grip and grabbed one hand and said, "Now, all the other introductions have to be easier than that one. So come on, big guy. Show me off."

Ben kissed her on the forehead and whispered in her ear, "This is why I love you, and the reason you are my love. Come on, and let me introduce you to everyone."

There were so many aunts, uncles, and cousins. Camille could not keep up with all the names. Everyone seemed so excited to meet her and were so funny. They all had a story about Ben or Benny, which was his childhood nickname. Camille thought it was adorable.

The older family members spoke on how remarkable he always was, and how they knew he was going to be something grand. The younger group told Camille how supportive he was as he showed up to school talent shows and sporting events. Whether it was little league or college level, Cousin Benny was there. The teenagers of the crowd called him uncle. That is what impressed Camille the most because that title is never given lightly in anybody's family. She felt like she knew firsthand about that because she had earned the right to be Nikki's Tee-Tee long before her dad had dropped the sibling bomb on her. Benjamin took special care in introducing Camille to Tabitha. Tabitha was Ben's cousin that Mother Ellen raised like a daughter after Mother Ellen's brother, Jerry, and his wife, Diana, passed away in a car crash. Tabitha lived with the Adams from the age of ten until she graduated college. She was introduced as his sister and Mother Ellen's oldest child. Tabitha was a few years older than Ben. She was married to a dentist, Dr. Ralph Jennings, and she worked as a dental hygienist in his practice. Tabitha and Ralph had a fifteen-year-old daughter, Kierra, who was a stunning scholar. She took to Camille right away, and when she found out Camille owned her own business, she never left her side. Camille warmed up to Kierra too. She promised to attend some of Kierra's debates with Ben and to come to some football games and parades to watch her strut her stuff as a member of the color guard. Camille was finding her place in Ben's family seemingly fine after Mrs. Carol went and sat in the corner.

Ben, however, was becoming more anxious by the moment. He started second guessing if he should ask Camille to marry him so publicly. What if she said no? What if she laughed in his face? What if mother Carol caused another scene? What if Paige, who looked like she was going to snap, caused a scene? There were so many what ifs that he did not hear his mother call the family into the dining room.

Kevin came up to him and said, "Yo, Ben, dinner is ready."

Everyone piled into the dining room grabbing a seat either at the adult table or one of the two kid's only tables. Ben's uncle, Jack, who was an elder at Liberty, led the family in prayer. Everyone held hands with bowed heads as Uncle Jack blessed the cook, partakers, children, pastor and wife (who were not present), the sick, the shut-in, Mayor A.C. Wharton, and President Obama. The prayer would have gone on until the food was cold had Ben not interjected with an "Amen, thanks, Uncle."

"The food prepared looks scrumptious," Ben told his mom.

She bashfully replied, "Thank you."

Camille could not believe the spread of food that was before them. Mother Ellen had something for everyone, from lean food for the calorie counters, gluten free for the diabetics, and fried food for those who were ready to chow down. The conversation was light and pleasant with laughter and smiles. Camille tried to shake off the death stares she was receiving from Mrs. Carol. She would not let her take away the joy of today's gathering. Camille reminded herself that all people grieved differently and needed time for healing. However, Paige leaned in and whispered to Camille, "That crazy lady looks like she is feeling some type of way down there. She better be cool because I'm about ready to snap her neck."

Camille loved Paige but could not have her flexing in Mother Carol's home. She whispered back to Paige, "I'm fine, don't worry about her."

Paige nodded and said, "But I got your back Mille, that's all I am saying."

"I know, girl, but stay cool, I'm fine." Camille looked at Karen and Frankie who were sitting across the table from her. They looked like a happy couple, and Camille's heart was warmed. Nikki was chatting it up with the other children at a kid's table. The dinner was nice and gave Camille a deep desire to have a family of her own. She was happy with the possibility it may happen one day.

As everyone was finishing their dessert, and coffee was being served, Benjamin stood and got everyone's attention by hitting his dessert knife on his glass. He rose and then said, "May I have your attention please?" Everything went quiet, and all eyes were focused on Ben as he stood in his, white crisp dress shirt and diamond cufflinks. His shirt was neatly tucked in his blue and white pin striped trousers. Camille swallowed hard because she was ogling the man as he was trying to make a family speech to end dinner, she guessed.

Ben cleared his throat and gave a nervous but heart–stopping smile. "Family, it has been great breaking bread with you today. It's been a minute since I've seen some of you, and I am happy to find that you all are doing well. I have been busy as usual for the last six months or so. Besides work, my time has been occupied by getting to know an extraordinary young lady." Ben turned and scanned the room. "You all have been introduced to her today." Ben walked to Camille and took her hands to help her stand up. "I want to say to Camille Danyelle James, six months ago, you stepped out of your SUV, and I instantly felt a connection. It was so strong that it took my breath away. It was not just your beauty, for I could not clearly see you that night, it was your spirit, your essence that traveled to greet me.

"Unfortunately, you were involved in an accident before we had a chance to speak face-to-face. That accident has led me to see what you were made of; you are made of the stuff that lasts forever. I have seen you overcome physical odds when the doctor said you might walk with a limp for the rest of your life. Your faith in

Jesus's healing powers and your tenacity allows you to wear those three-inch heels you should not be in." Chuckles were heard all over the room. "I have watched you have courage, strength, and all while running a company from your bed. You are a friend like none other, this I know, because your friends have never left your side, and that is why I asked them here today. Camille, you have turned my dark life into a bright sun shining day. I love you with God's love. I love you as his Word commands me to love a wife. I love you as I love myself. I am willing to die for you, to live with you, and I want to have you carry my name, carry my children inside your body, and share my life until I no longer have breath to breathe. Camille James, will you marry me?"

Camille could not believe the words coming out of Benjamin's mouth. The tears, the trembles, the snot, would not stop. Benjamin was really on one knee in front of his entire family and all their friends, asking for her hand in marriage. Not one romantic book she had ever read was as sweet as this. She felt as if she was outside of her body, her mind and heart were screaming "Yes! Oh,

Yes!" But nothing was coming out. She looked around and saw Karen, Mother Ellen, Paige, Tabitha and everyone else with tears streaming down their faces.

Paige finally said, "Camille, don't leave the man hanging, answer him already." There was laughter all around.

Camille finally came to her senses, lowered to her knees and said, "Yes, Benjamin George Adams, I will marry you." They kissed on the lips and hugged each other tightly as applause was heard all around them.

No one noticed until it was too late that Mrs. Carol had come up behind Ben—and knocked him in the head with an iron skillet from the kitchen. Ben toppled over, and Mrs. Carol stood screaming, "No! You can't have him! What about my Lauren?"

Mrs. Carol started charging for Camille, who was down checking on Benjamin. Uncle Jack and Frankie took the skillet from her and dragged her into another room.

Mother Ellen was screaming, "The Blood of Jesus, The Blood of Jesus!" The remainder of the house went up in pandemonium. Kevin had to grab Paige who was running after Mrs. Carol and the men carrying her, screaming obscenities. Karen went to help by getting an ice pack for Benjamin until the paramedics arrived. Tabitha had placed the 9-1-1 call.

Camille could not believe one minute she was saying yes to the love of her life, and the next he was out cold. What was with the pivotal moments of their lives? Their first date, she gets hit by a car. Their engagement, Ben gets knocked out by his deceased girlfriend's mother. *Was the Lord sending warning signs? Saying, Danger do not enter! Yield, proceed with Caution! It could be an enormous mistake, stop!* Camille was snapped out of her thoughts when she heard the sirens. The paramedics and police were there. The sirens also stirred Ben. He began to wake and immediately grabbed his head. Camille took his hand. He glanced at her, smiling. "You said yes." That one sentence gave Camille the peace she needed to know he was alright, and this was right.

The paramedics rushed in and took Ben's vitals and examined his head. Because he was out for over five minutes and had experienced trauma to the head, they took him to the emergency room to be examined as a precaution. Camille and Mother Ellen rode with him in the ambulance. The entire ride, the paramedic, John, asked Benjamin pertinent questions such as his name, birthday, and who the president was. When John asked him what today was, he answered, "The happiest day of my life. My lady said yes." The entire crew and mother Ellen laughed out loud.

John looked to a blushing but concerned Camille and asked, "Are you his lady?"

"Yes," she proudly answered. John shook his head, never had he seen starstruck lovers before, until now.

A couple of hours later, Benjamin, Camille, and Mother Ellen were being told all the scans looked good, and there were no signs of blood clots, swelling, or ruptures, and he was free to go. They advised him if he had any headaches that caused blurry vision or dizziness to go to the Emergency Room immediately. Benjamin agreed, and they all waited for Kevin to arrive to drive them home. Benjamin had already decided he would not press charges against Mrs. Carol. She was still grieving and in shock. Camille did not care for that decision, but what could she do. Mother Ellen agreed Mrs. Carol needed time to adjust. However, it wasn't lost on Camille that neither of them asked her what she thought.

*****

Kevin and Paige were on their way to the hospital to pick up Benjamin and the ladies. Kevin was the only person who could calm Paige down. She was set on slapping that crazy heifer for hitting Ben and charging at Camille. Karen, Tabitha, and Benjamin's aunts and cousins tried to tell Paige that Mrs. Carol was still hurting over the loss of her only daughter. Paige could not care less.

Paige yelled, "Well, I'm about to make her hurt over the pain in her eye when I sock her in it. She won't be thinking about her daughter or anybody else."

Kevin had to forcefully pull Paige away from the room Mrs. Carol was in. He grabbed her by the shoulders to face her toward him. Then he looked her eye to eye and said, "Paige you have to calm down. Fighting will not help Benjamin or Mrs. Carol. You are scaring the children and their parents, so stop this now!"

That got Paige to quiet down and take a seat. Kevin held her while she shook with tremors. Paige became quiet and balled up in a fetal position shaking as if she were in Alaska. Kevin rocked her in his arms until she was back to his Paige.

Now Paige sat quietly on the passenger's side of Kevin's car, wondering what happened. Again she had lost time and could not recall in detail the events of the evening. All she remembered was someone trying to hurt her best friend . . . her family and that was not allowed. She was grateful Kevin was there, if he wasn't, who knows what she would have done. She leaned over and rested her head on Kevin's shoulder. He turned and kissed the top of her head. How he loved this unpredictable and crazy woman.

****

"Now I lay me down to sleep; I pray the Lord, my soul to keep.

Keep me safe through the night and wake me with the morning light.

If I should die before I wake, I pray for Lord my soul to take. Amen"

Frankie and Karen were kneeling with Nikki beside her bed saying her good night prayers. It was the first night they did this as a family unit. Nikki's Sunday school teacher taught her class the prayer over the last few Sundays, and Nikki had been faithful. Frankie was overtaken by his emotions as he kissed his baby girl's forehead, and she said, "Night Daddy, I love you." He let the tears fall on her forehead, and she wiped them away looking at him curiously but remained quiet. It was as if she knew her daddy had come to the conclusion that he could not take leaving her any longer. He wanted to be there every night to say her prayers, and every morning to thank God for a brand new day.

Karen hugged and kissed Nikki. She rubbed Frankie's back to give him comfort. She could see he was struggling with his emotions but did not know in what direction he would be going. It had been such a long day. With the powerful worship service, and their talk on the way to Mother Ellen's, where they decided they would put the brakes on intimacy until marriage, and the fiasco after the proposal, it would take time for her to process it all. When they made it to the living room, they sat side by side on the couch.

Frankie blurted out, "I can't do this."

Karen's heart fell through her stomach. It had not been twenty-four hours yet. Was his emotional breakdown because he was walking away from her and Nikki without even trying? Karen felt her flesh wanting to say, *forget abstinence if it will make you stay*. She mentally told Satan to get behind her, and that thought left as quickly as it came. She slowly asked, "You cannot do what, Frankie?"

It felt like time stood still. Their short time as a family flashed before her eyes like a movie trailer. But then her heart rejoiced as the words Frankie spoke became audible to her.

"Karen, I cannot continue to tuck our baby girl in and go back home like some young man. I am forty-two years old. I am too old to date. I know you are my future. You, Nikki, Dawn, and Autumn are my family and my world. I want to marry you as soon as possible. We can go to marriage counseling, but I don't need a *how to date my woman* class. I need you emotionally and physically, and I am ready to marry you as soon as you will have me. So, tell me that you are ready to say yes to our family— say yes to us."

Karen leaped on Frankie screaming, "Yes, Lord! Thank you, Jesus! Yes! Frankie, I was so scared you were going to break up with me and walk out on Nikki when you were having your moment in there. Jesus, I was so scared."

Frankie grabbed Karen's hands and put them on the sides of her face. Then he took one hand and brushed her tears away. He tilted her head up and said, "Karen, I am never leaving you, ever. Well, I will leave tonight and each night until we are married. But, I am never walking out on you two."

Karen kissed him, and they held each other tight for minutes. They both told each other they loved one another and agreed to speak to the counselor at Liberty on Tuesday night about attending marriage counseling. They would be taking their vows as soon as possible.

Frankie stopped the conversation and said, "Karen, after we talk to the counselor on Tuesday, and you still want to proceed. We will go pick you out a wedding ring that will tell the world that you have been touched by my love." Karen happily agreed, and Frankie scooped her up in his arms and gave her a twirl. Karen giggled like she was a three-year-old, instead of the mother of one. Frankie bent down and gave her a lingering kiss then abruptly stopped and said, "Let me get out of here before we have to call the pastor tonight to marry us. Come walk me out, love."

Karen walked him to the front door and said, "Good night," as she closed the door. Then she did the cha-cha and started screaming, "I am getting married! I am getting married!"

Chapter 6: Love, Honor, and Respect

"Karen, that is the tenth dress you have tried on, pick one already!" Paige screamed at Karen as she frowned while looking in the mirror at her. Camille was standing by Karen's side straightening out the bottom of the silver dress Karen was trying on. The ladies were out shopping for Karen's wedding dress and their bridesmaid dresses.

Karen turned to face Paige and put one hand on her hip. "What is your problem, Paige? If you don't want to be here, then go home. I am fine with just having Camille, Dawn, and Autumn as my bridesmaids. You are dismissed because I am sick and tired of your pouting!"

"Ladies, let's calm down, no one is going anywhere," Camille said firmly. "Paige, you have been a pain all day. We understand it is because you are in limbo right now with Kevin. But that is your own doing."

Paige gasped. "What do you mean my own doing?"

Camille chuckled and shook her head while she watched Karen take a twirl in the dress like Kenya Moore, the former Miss USA and reality TV star on Atlanta Housewives. Paige stepped in front of Camille rolling her neck and eyes. "Mille, what do you mean my own doing?"

"Paige, you are the one that went to Atlanta and beat Kevin's mother up like you're *Straight Outta Compton*. Now, I am not saying Julia was not out of line, she was. But, sweetie, you have got to start taking responsibility for you and your alter ego, Raige's actions." Karen burst out into laughter with Camille.

Paige was furious. "How dare you take that evil woman's side? She spat in my face what was I to do?"

Karen chimed in on that question. "You were to take a step back and ask yourself if beating her down was worth you losing Kevin. That is what you were supposed to do. Then you should have told Kev, and his daddy, so they could deal with her. If you had done that, you would not be here ruining this great girls' day out. We are planning my wedding, and we are supposed to be happy!"

Karen rolled her eyes, then looked at Camille and said, "This is the one." Camille jumped up and down with Karen as they chanted, "We are getting married, we are getting married."

Paige stepped out of the dressing area and sat on a nearby couch. She had to admit; Raige was out and in rare form. If she were to have an honest moment with herself, Karen was speaking the truth. There was another way she could have dealt with Julia, but she just could not see herself letting that woman or anyone else walk all over her. Why should she have run to Kevin like she could not take care of herself? The sensible Paige took over and said, *so you won't lose the best man that ever happened to you. So you can have a girls' day out in the future where you can try on ten dresses and get on Karen's nerves.*

Raige did not like those thoughts and cut in. *Yeah, and see how long Kevin will want a weak woman.*

Sensible Paige said, *Kevin just wants me to stop reacting negatively to his mother's antics.*

She recalled Sunday night when Kevin came into her apartment. They spoke, and he put all his cards on the table for her. Tears rolled down her cheeks, and she wiped them angrily as the memory played back in her mind.

Kevin was holding Paige, stroking her hair as her head laid on his chest. She looked up at him and said, "Why can't we stay like this? The two of us together without the outsiders ruining everything?"

Kevin raised Paige up gently and responded. "Paige, outsiders are not ruining us; we are ruining us."

Paige jumped to speak, but Kevin put his index to her lips and continued. "I love you, Paige, with all of my heart, but for us to be together, you have got to get your anger in check. I know my mother was wrong, and Ms. Carol was wrong, but you have got to learn how to respond in an appropriate manner. I am an Assistant D. A., and I will not have a girlfriend ruining my career because she cannot control her temper. I am willing to work with you in counseling. I will continue to go to Liberty Church if that will help us. This church thing is really working for the others. But what I will not tolerate is any more acts of violence from you, do you understand me?"

Paige was at a loss for words; she really could not answer him. She had been protecting herself all of her life. How else could she preserve her dignity when people crossed the line?

Kevin stood up breaking her trance and pulled her up too. He kissed her temple and said, "You don't have to answer me tonight. Get some rest and call me when you are ready to move our relationship forward. Otherwise, I guess we are ruined, and I don't want that but will accept it."

Paige could not move as she accepted his lingering kiss and watched him stroll out of her apartment and possibly, out of her life.

Now, six days later, Paige sat ruining their girls' day out with her bad attitude. All because Kevin remained true to his word, he did not call her all week, and she could not let go of her stubborn pride to reach out. She saw him on Wednesday when everyone went to

Benjamin's to celebrate the two engagements. Benjamin was doing well. He had no injuries from being hit with the skillet. She still wanted to knock Mrs. Carol on her behind for that one. That night gave Paige a dose of what it would be like without Kevin. He acted as if she was invisible. Kevin spoke to her saying hello, and then, later on, good-bye. She missed him sorely but did not know how to let go of her own stubborn will.

"Paige, are you coming with us?" Camille asked her, breaking her thoughts. "We have checked out, and now, Karen wants to go to Owen Brennan's for an early dinner."

Paige got up and walked to the girls. "I am sorry for my attitude, Karen and Mille. I have to go and think some things through. You both go on without me, and enjoy the rest of the day." Paige walked off without allowing them to respond. She pulled out her phone, activated Siri, and said, "Call Kev's mobile."

"Hello."

"Hi, Kevin, it's Paige. Can I come meet you?"

"Sure, love, I'm at the office."

Hope sprang in her heart as he called her love, she would not ruin them. "I am on my way."

****

"Paul, I am sorry to hear Brian is going to have to do that much time. But man, the young lady he hit and left could have died."

Frankie truly regretted Brian letting the alcohol, and whatever other substance he took that night, overtake him. Although his friend Paul called to update him on Brian's case, Frankie was already aware of the ruling and subsequent sentence. He was there when Kevin revealed it to them at Benjamin's house when they celebrated the engagements. The ladies came up with that idea of a double engagement party. It was nice. Everyone, including Frankie, was relieved that Brian was to serve five years. However, Paul was unaware of the connection he had with the victim through his now fiancée and baby daughter. Paul ended the conversation with Frankie stating he just wanted him to know. Frankie thanked him and disconnected.

Frankie took a seat on his sofa to watch some SEC Football. Alabama was playing Ole Miss, and he hated not being at The Grove for game day. However, he was expecting his bride-to-be to be back after shopping with the girls. He smiled thinking about the last week. Dawn and Autumn were ecstatic for him and Karen. They agreed to be in the wedding and were out with Nikki taking her to the Children's Museum and lunch at her favorite restaurant. He thought about how God had given him a new life. It could have easily been him looking at a five-year bid. He could not have a job, a family, and friends because he was an alcoholic and drug abuser, But God! Frankie's thoughts were interrupted by his mobile device buzzing. It was Shayla. He had not talked to her in a couple of weeks. He wondered if the girls had shared the news of his pending nuptials for the following Saturday. He gave Karen two weeks to make it happen, and he was serious. On the third ring, he answered bracing himself for the overdue round with Shayla Yvonne Jones.

"Hello."

"Frankie, I am going to see you at church tomorrow, right?"

"And good morning to you, Ms. Jones, how are you?"

"Cut the crap, Frankie, and answer the question."

"Shayla, I will be attending Liberty Fellowship tomorrow as I have become a member."

"You have got to be kidding me! Frankie what about me and our daughters? We have been attending church together for years. You told me it was the least you could do for all the hell you took us through. Now, that doesn't mean anything?"

"Shayla, of course, it means something. I am eternally grateful for our friendship. However, I have done all that I know to do to make amends for the hurt I caused you and our daughters. I will not feel guilty for moving on with Karen and the family we have created. They are my future."

"Wow, so just forget about us?"

"Shayla, my girls are part of my future. They are in the wedding. At this very moment, they are out bonding with their little sister."

"So, you just have everything, huh? You treat me miserably for years, then get yourself together and make a new family. One you didn't know about for three years. Now, you do, and you just take my girls and everything away from me."

"Shayla, you are talking nonsense. Dawn and Autumn are not being taken from you. They are adults and can share in both our worlds. What is wrong with you?"

"You, Frankie. You are what is wrong with me. I am still in love you. I want our family back. Nikki can be a part of our family. I will love her because she is a part of you. But I will not accept you leaving me, leaving us behind."

"Shayla! There. Is. No. Us! Get yourself together! We have been divorced for six years. When I got out of rehab and was clean for a year, I asked if you wanted to try again. You told me no. Now, you bring this family crap to me. We are friends. I am in love with Karen, and we are getting married next Saturday."

"Frankie, don't you scream at me. You know why I couldn't marry you again. But we made love whenever you wanted. That is all I had to give you then. I can give you more now. Please, let's try. Karen is too young for you. It won't work. What if she does drugs again? She will bring you down with her, and all your progress will be ruined."

"Shayla, my sobriety is not in jeopardy with Karen. Now, I am done with this conversation. Please don't look for me tomorrow or any other Sunday. I have moved on. I apologize for my having sex with you over the years. I see my actions led you to believe that I was not looking for more, and for the longest time I wasn't. But now, I have more, and it is with Karen. I hope you can understand. Goodbye, Shayla." Frankie swiped the phone to end the call. He said, "Lord, help her." Then he picked up the remote and tuned into the game.

Shayla sat on the other side of the ended call crying and swearing at Frankie Lee Jones. She called Dawn and got her voicemail, then called Autumn who picked up. Shayla lit into the girl, calling her and her sister traitorous, ungrateful spawns. She vowed to make them all pay. She disconnected the call with Autumn and gathered herself to the point of psychotic calm as she began to plot to make sure Frankie and Karen's marriage never happened. Frankie and their daughters would pay for this betrayal.

****

After leaving the restaurant on her drive to Benjamin's, Camille could not believe what a coward she had been. She would not admit to herself that she did not bring up the possibility that she and Karen could be sisters out of fear. She rationalized with herself that she did not want to deflate Karen's day any more than Paige had already. Karen was the happiest she had ever seen her. What would the knowledge of a shared father do to their bond? Would she be overjoyed that they were sisters? Would she blame her for not being able to get their dad to stick around? As Camille watched Karen take a phone call from Frankie's twin daughters, and Nikki, Karen was glowing as Nikki expressed how much fun they had at the Children's Museum. Camille resolved that she would wait until after their honeymoon to bring up this family dilemma to Karen. She also wanted to get Benjamin's take on the situation. Camille was pulling up to Benjamin's enormous home located on Southwind Golf Course to see her fiancé. She was just coming to terms that, in the next year, she would be somebody's wife and could start working on becoming a mommy. God was indeed good to her despite all the hiccups that had been occurring. She used the garage door opener Ben gave her and drove into his three-car garage. She found Benjamin in his home study. When she knocked on the door, he immediately rose to greet her with a warm embrace, a kiss on the forehead, and a light kiss on the lips. Benjamin took her hands and led her to the love seat in his office while he pulled a chair to sit across from her.

"How did you enjoy your girls' day out, sweetie?"

"It was great, well after we got Paige's attitude in check. She was a royal pain with her pouting, but we handled it, and she apologized. We actually found Karen's dress and ours. Only Karen and I went to lunch. Paige, I assume, went to patch things up with Kevin."

Ben raised an eyebrow and gave an incredulous look. "Do you think that is wise?"

Camille shrugged. "I don't know, Ben. They are a mess together, but Paige is a bigger mess without him. I am just praying that they both seek the Lord and try to find common ground whether it's them being together or just being friends."

"Yeah, you are right. I just don't want anything bad happening." Ben looked at Camille as she started rubbing her forehead and shaking her leg. He knew this was a nervous habit of hers.

"Babe, is Paige and Kevin's relationship bothering you this much? You seem nervous."

"No, it's not their relationship that has me troubled."

"Is it us? I know we have had some hard times lately, and Carol's crazy attempt to knock me out did not help. But mom and I are going to get her the help she needs."

It was Camille's turn to give an incredulous look. "I can understand Mother Ellen helping her friend, but why are you involved? That lady could have killed you."

"Because I owe it to Lauren, to make sure her mother heals."

"What if she does not want to be healed? What if she just wants you to stay single, hurting, and mourning over Lauren with her for the rest of your life?"

"Camille, I have to try. Please don't give me resistance on this. I have found my soul mate in you, and Carol's only child can't be replaced."

"I understand that, but there are medical professionals and other members of the church that can assist her. Besides, if Paige did not stop her, I would have been next on her injury list. Paige also may lose Kevin because she snapped trying to defend me. All because

Mrs. Carol lost her daughter and did not want you to move on."

"Babe, I owe it to her, and I am going to help her."

"Benjamin, she physically hurt you!"

"It doesn't matter; I forgive her. I owe her this."

"Fine. Then you pay your debts to your mother-in-law, and I will just go home and deal with my family issues on my own."

"Camille, she is not my mother-in-law, but I did date her daughter for seven years. Please understand, and what family issues are you referring to, Paige and Kevin?"

"No, it's not Paige or Kevin. Although, I am worried what a permanent break up will do to Paige. But, don't you worry about my family issues. I came over to share them with you, but I see your dedication lies with your dead girlfriend and her crazed mother, so I will leave you to paying your debts to them." Camille knew that was low. He had hurt her feelings, and she wanted to hurt his.

Ben jumped in shock at that statement. "Camille, how can you say that? I just want to make sure Carol is okay. I love you, and I am dedicated to you for the rest of my life."

"Whatever, Ben. Call me when you have time to talk to your living fiancée. I will not live in Lauren's shadow. Nor will I sit by while you babysit a grown woman who can't understand that just because you love me. That. Is. A. Negative." Camille grabbed her purse and headed for the garage. Ben ran after her.

"Camille, wait a minute. What's going on? No one is more important than you. I just want to help Carol. But that does not change that I want to be here for you."

"Ben, you can't handle everything, and the fact that you have told me, 'don't give you resistance' lets me know that I'm not first in your life, no matter what you say." Camille jerked her arm away, got into her car, and backed up, letting the garage door up and then back down once she backed out. She turned her radio up loud and screamed, "Forget him!"

Benjamin pressed the garage door opener and ran down his driveway trying to stop her. Camille was gone. The taillights of her SUV were barely visible. This was not what he planned for this evening. He would have to rethink his involvement in Carol's treatment. When he agreed to help his mother, he did not think it would be a risk to his relationship with Camille. Nothing—no one was worth Camille being angry with him. He grimaced at the thought of losing her. In a matter of months, she had captured his heart and mind. She was the answer to his prayers, and he could not mess this up. Clearly, she was dealing with something. But what family issues? Her only biological connection was Mr. James who was back in the Middle East. Ben pulled out his mobile device and called Karen.

****

Paige knocked on Kevin's office door. Due to it being Saturday, the lobby area where his assistants worked was clear. She did not get a response, so she decided just to go in. He couldn't be far. She had called ahead, and he knew she was on her way. As she entered his small but organized office, she shook her head at how everything was perfectly positioned and in the right place. His degrees, awards, newspaper articles, and magazine features were on one wall screaming how accomplished he was. He had two wall bookshelves with law books and other literature that Paige was sure he had read a time or two. His large desk was oak and had family pictures with his mom and dad. In the center of his desk was a notepad with an ink pen and his laptop. On the other side of his laptop was a picture of Paige and Kevin, she could not remember what function they were attending. The look in Kevin's eyes was one of admiration and love. As Paige looked around his office, she began to think of how Kev liked attention to detail. How everything had a place and belonged in that place. She felt guilt overtake her gut and spread throughout her body. She could not continue to be this out of control and out of place obstacle in his neat world. How had he put up with her for three years? It was no longer any wonder to her, why she had not received the ring she found almost a year ago. She did not deserve it. She was out of place in his life. Paige turned to leave before Kevin came into his office. She needed more time to contemplate if she could truly be what Kevin needed. When she turned around, Kevin had entered the room behind her with McAlister's bags, and sweet tea in his hands, her favorite. Kevin looked adorable in his khaki pants and white Ralph Lauren golf shirt with khaki Sperry shoes. How could she hold on to him?

Kevin tried to maintain his composure as he motioned for Paige to have a seat at the table in his office. After she'd called, he rushed out to get them lunch. He knew how much Paige loved McAlister's chicken tortilla soup, with a turkey club on a croissant, and sweet tea. He got her a chocolate chip cookie as well, although he knew she would nibble on it for hours because she would feel guilty but enjoy that sinful pleasure. Sinful pleasure—that was what Paige was to him. He missed her something bad but knew she was an explosive that could ruin his career and family. But without his little dynamite, his world was empty. He needed her. She had to get help with her anger issues. He had worked too hard and long to become the man he was in the community. Bloggers had started to comment on his feisty girlfriend. Normally, that would not bother him, but he wanted to run for District Attorney in the next election. How could he do that if one day he would have to prosecute his own woman for battery? As he finished setting up their lunch, he grabbed her hands and said grace. While eating, they made small talk and then there was silence for some time. Kevin decided to address the elephant in the room.

"So, Paige, why did you decide to come see me today? Are you ready to address our last conversation?"

"I thought I was," Paige said with a whisper. "But now I don't know."

"What's changed since the phone call?"

"Coming into your office, seeing how everything is where it belongs. You are a perfectionist Kevin, and I am a ticking time bomb. I don't want to ruin your career or cause problems in your family. But I just don't know how else to protect myself." Tears flowed down Paige's face with such force they were unstoppable. She dropped her head on the table and cried in the crook of her arm.

Kevin got out of his chair and walked around to kneel at Paige's feet. He lifted her arms off the table and cupped her chin. Paige's eyes were closed, but the tears continued to flow. She looked like a vulnerable baby china doll, like the ones in his mother's collection. Paige was his vulnerable baby china doll, once again. Paige was exploding before him, but this explosion made him want to run to her and shield her from harm.

"Paige, I love you, baby doll. I am here to protect you. I just need you to come to me. Let me know when someone, anyone, including my mother, has come at you wrong. I will help you fight every battle. I won't leave you, baby. I won't let harm come to you. I need you trust that. Can you?"

"Kevin, I want to. I really do, but what if I can't? I know your career is in the public eye, and you need a woman that is not like me." Kevin wiped Paige's tears from her cheeks, pulled her up so he could sit down and placed her on his lap. She turned to him fighting back more tears. Her heart was breaking over the fact that she may lose the best man because of her lack of trust.

"Paige, I just need you to try. I don't want what we have to end. I have been miserable without you. You bring excitement to my boring legal life. You bring me comfort with your warm embraces, and you bring happiness to my heart with your quick wit and bubbly personality. It's just when you come blazing at people, and to your credit, it is to defend yourself or the ones you love. However, kicking butt and taking names does not work, sweetie. It must stop. You have to get help with your anger issues."

Paige took in every word Kevin spoke to her. He was gentle and kind. She wanted to try—she had to try. There would never be another love like this. She would never find anyone else to see the true Paige. She had to work on herself.

"I will, Kevin. I will get help. I will find a therapist to talk with and continue to go to church. I love you, Kevin, and I don't want to lose you."

"I am here, baby doll. I'm always here for you."

"Kevin."

"Baby doll."

"Can I have my cookie now?" Paige gave him the sweetest smile.

"How do you know I have a cookie for you?" Kevin stood her on her feet so that he could get up.

"Because you love me, and you know what I like." Kevin pulled the huge chocolate cookie from the carryout bag, unwrapped the cookie, and fed it to his girl. Paige moaned as she savored the chewy delight.

Kevin bent down and kissed her on the forehead, then whispered in her ear. "I think we will make it, and I miss you moaning that way. Come home with me now." They left Kevin's office, and Paige followed him home where she spent the night causing the kind of explosions Kevin could handle.

Karen and Frankie's Wedding

"One more with just the bride and groom." The photographer called out to the wedding party. Camille walked behind Karen, Paige, Dawn, and Autumn as she scooped up Nikki who was whining because of the long day. She smiled as she looked at Karen and Frankie who had just been married by a judge in a small garden at the Memphis Botanical Garden. Karen was radiant in her silver mermaid gown. The wedding was beautiful and intimate. Camille thought Frankie's daughters were wonderful. They were true identical twins. She could not find one difference in them. Ben came up behind her tugging on her hair while playing peekaboo with Nikki. Camille turned to see who was pulling her hair and stirring up Nikki, who had just started to rest with her head on her shoulder. When she saw it was Ben, she smiled.

"Hey, don't stir her up. This day is getting to her, and we still have the reception in the Goldsmith's room."

Ben shrugged his shoulders and kept messing with Ms. Shopkin, as he called her, and pinched her nose. Camille gave him a maternal stare down that meant *stop it or else*. Ben raised his hands in surrender. "Fine, I will behave. How are you doing, honey? We haven't talked much lately."

Camille took a deep breath. She wanted to stay angry with him after their blow up a week ago. They had both been busy and had not seen each other much. Only the past Wednesday at Bible Study, and last night at the rehearsal dinner. It was not uncommon for them to go several days without seeing one another because of her responsibility to ITS, and his obligations to work. However, this was the first time their relationship to felt strained.

"I'm fine. Just working, keeping up with my physical therapy exercises, and helping Karen with the wedding. It was beautiful don't you agree?"

"Yes, it was lovely, but I know who will make a more beautiful bride."

"Oh, do you, now?" Camille could not let go of the sarcasm. She did not know why she felt threatened by him helping Ms. Carol. It just seemed like a betrayal, and she could not shake it off.

"Yes, I do, and I am looking at the bride–to–be right now."

"Well, we will see," Camille said sharply and put Nikki down as the photographer asked for the daughters to join in the pictures.

This was Benjamin's time to get through to Camille. She had given him nothing but shade since their argument. Wednesday night he tried to speak to her, but she gave him the cold shoulder. Last night, he sat by her at the rehearsal dinner, but she tended to Nikki as though she was an infant rather than the big girl she was. He smiled as he recalled Ms. Shopkin's screaming in her god-aunt's face.

"Tee-Tee, I can feed myself."

Camille had no choice but to move on to being a nursemaid to Karen. When Karen shooed her away, she then moved on to nervously picking up trash and refilling the guest's beverages, which was absurd because Frankie and Karen had hired a caterer and servers. The woman was acting so out of character, and it was beginning to get on his nerves. He took her gently by the elbow and led her into the building, walking briskly.

"Ben, slow down. Why are you dragging me around?"

"Because I don't deserve this shade you are giving me, it ends now."

"What shade are you talking about, Ben? And don't manhandle me again."

"You know what I am talking about. This is not how we will treat one another when we don't agree on something. We will talk about whatever is between us like mature, loving, Christian adults."

"Ben, this is not the time for that. This is my sis— I mean, best friend's wedding day. I will not allow the ghost of Lauren to loom over it." Camille tried walking away. She could see the rest of the wedding party lining up, and the guests had begun coming inside. Ben would not let her go. She was not feeling all that Christian at the moment and needed for him to back off.

"Camille, I am not letting you go until you listen to me."

"This is not the time to talk about this. I am going to line up with the wedding party as you should be doing too. We can talk later." She wiggled her way out of his grip and made a mad dash to the wedding line.

Benjamin stood there exasperated. He was going to put an end to this standoff of hers. For goodness sake, he was just trying to help someone. Where was her compassion, and what had her stumbling over who Karen was?

"Women!" Ben walked and stood behind Kevin in the wedding processional shaking his head.

"Tee-Tee and Ms. Paige, my mommy and daddy are married. We gone live in my daddy's house, and my big sisters are going to come see me all the time. You all can come over too and have fun."

Camille and Paige laughed and hugged Nikki. They were both so happy for Karen's life and excited for Nikki to have a shot at a complete family. They were all waiting to walk into the Goldsmith's room as the bride and groom were making their entrance. Nikki was between Camille and Paige, and they were swinging her by the arms. Nikki was having a ball being a human swing and was giggling causing everyone around to smile. All of a sudden, they heard a loud shriek and ran in to see what the noise was.

Karen wiped the tears from her eyes as she saw the servers trying to save her beautiful wedding cake. Her day had been perfect. She woke up at The Peabody Hotel, where she received a makeover courtesy of Camille with a massage. She rode in a limo to the Botanical Gardens and married the man of her dreams, and the father of her child, while the sun set in, front of their guests. For late August in Memphis, the weather was unseasonably cool, only eighty degrees. The outside ceremony was perfect. The judge Kevin had suggested did a wonderful job with their vows. Due to Frankie being married before and them having a child, they did not want Pastor Caine to fill obligated to marry them. They were not the traditional couple, and she was fine with the judge. Pastor Caine and his wife attended the ceremony, though.

But now she was heartbroken that her three-tier cake had fallen apart. The caterer could not say why it was falling apart. That maybe the cakes were not cool enough to hold the icing. It looked like a melting sweet volcano, as it had chocolate, white, and red velvet cakes on each level. The cake maker had come highly recommended and made thousands of cakes a year. She was sure it was not incompetence that caused the cake avalanche. Besides, as she inspected the cake, it looked like the cake was pushed over. Who would want to destroy someone's wedding cake?

She was snapped out of her thoughts and silenced from screaming, by realizing she was audibly sobbing. She turned and fell into Frankie's arm whimpering. He stroked her back lightly and whispered comforting words into her ear.

"Karen, the cake is still edible. No reason to allow that to ruin our night, okay." Karen knew he was right, but that did not stop the tears. Dawn and Autumn came up to comfort her too, asking if she needed to go out to get some fresh air. She told them she was okay, and she and Frankie could proceed to the bride and groom's table.

Karen tried her best to shake off the feeling that her cake disaster was not a coincidence, something just felt off. And that included Camille, who had been acting so clingy the last couple of weeks, beyond the point of being a great maid of honor.

Karen had tried talking to her after the phone call with Ben. She definitely understood why Camille would be concerned about Ben being involved in Ms. Carol's life. That lady was a nut case attacking Ben, then attempting to attack Camille. Ben had informed Karen that Camille mentioned family issues. She could only think that maybe Camille just missed Mr. James. He had stayed several weeks while she healed, which was the longest span of time he had ever visited since she had known Camille. When she asked her what Ben was referring to, Camille said it was nothing, and they would talk after her honeymoon. Surely, something that could wait two weeks was not that dire, so Karen remained quiet. But something was definitely going on with Camille. Karen again was pulled out of her thoughts as

Camille and Paige came to sit with her. Paige was beaming as she reached over and gave Karen a hug.

"So, Ms. Lady, you're married now. I am so happy for you." Paige stepped aside so Camille could give Karen a hug.

"You know I am happy for you too, Karen," Camille said while hugging Karen.

"Thank you both. I am so grateful. You both have been there for me over the years when I was a struggling single mom. I can't believe we pulled this wedding off in just two weeks. I appreciate you, girls, more than you know. I would not be here if it were not for you."

Paige chimed in. "Girl, you know we got you. Besides, who knew we would find your baby's daddy delivering mail at Kev's office. What were the chances of that? Something good came out of Camille being hit by that SUV."

Camille just rolled her eyes, only Paige could say something caring, then follow it up with something so off. Karen frowned at Paige. "I thought you were working on yourself. You know, trying to show Kevin you were sophisticated."

Paige gave a smirk. "I am a work in progress, besides Mille knows what I mean." Paige looked at Camille for confirmation.

"Paige, you are fine. I am happy the driver is locked away for some time. I am healing fine, and Karen has found love. All is perfect."

It was Paige's turn to frown. "If all is perfect, then why do you have poor Benjamin looking like he has lost his best friend?"

Sometimes, Camille really wanted to deck Paige. "Ben and I are fine, Paige. You just work on your attitude, so Kevin will finally give you that ring he has had for over a year."

Camille gave Paige a wink, and a look that Paige knew meant she was about to cross the line with her mouth. "Oh, look at who needs some lessons in etiquette."

Before Camille or Karen could utter a word, Frankie came over and took Karen's hand and said,

"Excuse me, ladies. I would like to have a dance with my wife." The ladies stood and let Karen go dance with her husband while the D.J. played "Here and Now" by Luther Vandross.

Kevin and Paige joined them on the dance floor. Ben had to pull Camille to the dance floor, but she finally relaxed and enjoyed the feel of his warm embrace. They swayed to the melody and lyrics—lyrics that rang true for all three couples. It talked about of looking into the eyes of one's mate and seeing what they mean to each other. It spoke of knowing and believing in your heart that the one you are with is the only person's love you will need. The dance floor was full of partners enjoying a night of love and celebration for the happy newlyweds. It was a night for new beginnings.

Chapter 7: Baggage Sunday

The altar at Liberty Fellowship Church was decorated with luggage of all sizes and colors. Camille looked up as she walked down the aisle and saw the suitcases displayed on stage. There were more in front of the choir and orchestra. She wondered, "What on earth has Pastor Caine planned today?"

Entering the row where Mother Ellen sat, she was greeted with a warm smile. Standing to the right of Mother Ellen was Mrs. Carol. Camille went to greet her while repeating in her head—*it's nice to be nice . . . it's nice to be nice.* However, she did not have to worry about speaking to the unfriendly woman. Mrs. Carol sat down and started rummaging through her purse to avoid talking to Camille.

Mother Ellen compensated for Mrs. Carol's less than Christian attitude. She took Camille's purse and bible case. "Daughter, that was some wedding you girls pulled off yesterday. It was beautiful. I can hardly wait to see what yours and Ben's will look like in a few months."

That brought out a genuine smile from Camille. She loved how Mother Ellen always referred to her as daughter. Before Camille could respond, Mrs. Carol looked up from her purse.

"Ellen, what are you talking about? I heard the cake fell apart. What is beautiful about that?" Mother Ellen's eyes bulged, and nostrils flared. Camille would not have her going there with Ms. Carol.

"Mother Ellen, you are so kind. I am happy Karen has what she deserves with Frankie and Nikki. They have both gone through so much. I pray they are satisfied with their day. I am certainly looking forward to planning our wedding, with your help, of course. I am honored Ben believes I am the one for him."

"Well, believe it, daughter, because it is true, and I believe it too. By the way, where is that son of mine?" Mother Ellen was turning and looking toward all the entrances for her son. Camille's eyes drifted up to the overhead monitor where the media team had the countdown clock displayed. It was twelve minutes until the service began. She had not spoken to Ben since he dropped her off last night.

"I am not sure where he is, let me text him. I am sure he is in the building somewhere." As she typed, her attention was drawn to Mrs. Carol who looked as if she had something to add to the "Where is Ben?" conversation.

"Maybe Ben would like to sit with just his two mothers today, me and Ellen. You have really inserted yourself everywhere in his life. There was a time, before you joined this church and stole him away, that Ben would sit between us. Maybe he has come to his senses, and this is a sign you need to back off!"

Mother Ellen turned and said, "Carol, that is enough! Ben can sit wherever he chooses, and he wants to sit near his fiancée. If you can't keep your responses to yourself, I suggest—you move!" Camille, frozen in her seat, sat facing forward unable to see how Mrs. Carol responded to the scolding. Her ears were burning from being caught off guard and insulted by Mrs. Carol's jab. How could this lady be so evil in the house of the Lord?

Camille looked around the nearly full to capacity sanctuary and spotted Paige near the back. She grabbed her purse and Bible. Mother Ellen tried to stop her, and she paused. Camille gathered her emotions and addressed her with as much respect as possible.

"Mother Ellen, please let me go. I will sit with Paige and Kevin. When Ben comes, just tell him where I am." She kissed Mother Ellen on the cheek and made a mad dash to sit with her best friend. As she greeted Paige, she tried to check her embarrassment and frustration in the aisle.

The service was to begin in five minutes when Camille noticed Ben entering to sit by his mother. She could not believe it when she saw Mrs. Carol moving over and motioning with her hands for Ben to sit down in between them. Paige, calling her name, interrupted her eye stalking.

"Camille, why are you back here, and Ben is up there?"

"Um, Err . . . I just wanted to sit with my BFF."

"Why?"

"Because, Paige, let's just enjoy the service. The praise and worship team is about to get started."

*****

Ben closed his eyes, as he stood singing "Amazing Grace" along with the Praise and Worship Team. He was considering partnering with the music ministry. He needed to use the gift of voice with which the Lord had blessed him. He was late entering the service because his Sunday school class went over the time allotted. They were discussing the life of Apostle Paul, and the time had escaped them. Had he known Camille would not sit in her normal seat, by him, he would have left class early. He thought when he texted her where he was she would have sat tight. Her absence was making it hard for him to focus on the worship in the auditorium. There was also something strange going on with his mom. She seemed to be in a bad mood. Not to mention, Mother Carol trying to make him sit in between them; he hated sitting in between them. He was a thirty-something-year-old man, for goodness sake. He suffered through months of that, after Lauren's death, and only because Mother Carol was grieving. However, enough was enough. The Lord had healed him and given him another chance at love. His mom and scripture taught him that Christians should bear one another's burdens, but he would not be holding Mrs. Carol's hand any longer.

When Elder John completed the welcome and said to go greet someone, he ran to Camille with his iPad in hand. Experiencing the worship service and God's word with his lady next to his side was how Ben had started each week for the last several months. Today would be no different. He entered the row and grabbed Camille's hand. Ben shook it as if she was the queen of England and sang the greeting song of Liberty to her.

"Good Morning, Sister. The Jesus in me loves the Jesus in you. The Jesus in me loves the Jesus in you, you're easy, so easy, you're easy, easy to love." Camille blushed. What could a girl do after that, but smile and enjoy the remainder of the service.

Paige watched the two lovebirds as the choir sang. She could not wait to get to the bottom of this musical chair act between Benjamin and Camille. However, for now, she had to key into the service. Kevin had given her notice that she had to change. More than his notice, Paige knew she needed to change. This was the best place for her to start. The choir was singing "This Is Holy Ground." Paige had to admit this choir could really sing.

No, it's the anointing, she thought. Paige smirked. Listen to me already feeling a shift within my spirit. She rose to her feet, pulled her hands together to her breast, and closed her eyes as she let the lyrics break up the fallow ground in her heart and mind.

> *This is Holy ground,*
> *we're standing on Holy ground*
> *For the Lord is here*
> *and where he is, is Holy*
> *This is holy ground,*
> *We're standing on Holy Ground*
> *For the Lord is here*
> *and where he is, is Holy*

We are standing on Holy ground.

And I know that these are angels all

around

Let us praise Jesus now

We are standing in Your presence, on

Holy ground.

With each visit to Liberty, Kevin was drawn into this Protestant way of worship and lifestyle. It was vastly different from his Catholic upbringing, but he could feel the presence of the angels that the choir just finished singing about. He was also blown away by the luggage on display. Kevin was anxiously anticipating what Pastor Caine would lecture about using luggage. In his bulletin, there was a note card with a question, "What is your baggage?"

Kevin likened the service to a college course. He supposed that this was the best way to deliver instructions that could be applied by anyone who heard. According to Elder John, all the services were televised and streamed online, so there could actually be millions of people hearing the word of God. Kevin sat up in his seat as Pastor Caine came on the stage with luggage chained to his body. The lead pastor was about to fall face forward, but he caught himself and began to deliver what Kevin, and most in attendance, considered a timely word. Pastor Caine delivered a message about "Traveling Light." He started.

"To do that in today's society is difficult because we are weighted down with baggage. There are four types of baggage: 1) Personal, 2) Work, 3) Church, 4) Other People's."

Kevin was intrigued by this analogy. Pastor Caine was on the mark with him when it came to personal and work baggage. He listened as Pastor Caine continued.

"As individuals, we try to be light and happy. We try to leave our unhappiness at the door. As the ushers escort us to our seats, we put on a smile trying to forget our failures, fears, and regrets but the personal baggage is stuck to us like glue. It is chained to us."

Kevin could agree to that in his mind, heart, and soul because his personal baggage was flowing over to his work baggage. It all was becoming too heavy, causing him both doubt and anxiety. As a public figure, he had to be transparent in all aspects of his life. Could he hold on to Paige and continue up the corporate ladder? Could he let go of the regret when perpetrators went free because of the negligence of his office, leaving victims hurting? He wanted to release these burdens, but another issue was plaguing his heart. He always understood Peter was the rock that we should lean on for strength to be the Christian example. This is what he learned from the nuns. Jesus told Peter, "Upon this Rock, I will build my church." Kevin shook that off. He assumed that was church baggage he needed to cast away. The more he attended the services and classes at Liberty; the more he believed that Jesus Christ himself was that rock.

As Kevin pondered those questions, Paige could do nothing but close her eyes as Pastor Caine continued the message that was nothing but the truth for her. Pastor Caine had one baggage for personal. Paige, if she was honest with herself, had dozens of personal baggage chained to her. As Pastor Caine explained how personal baggage came to be, he was telling the story of her life. Her baggage began before she could remember. Her mother was addicted to drugs, causing her to care for herself as a toddler. That began her need for self–preservation, by any means necessary, to take root. Add to that every family hurt, including being sexually violated, verbally abused and continually neglected— Paige was left chained and bound. Tears began to stream as she received Pastor Caine's words of redemption.

He explained, 1 Peter 5:7. *"Cast all your anxiety on him because he cares for you."* Paige repeated that last phrase silently to herself. "He cares for me." She had a heavenly father that cared for her, and who wanted her baggage. Instantly, her mind went to Kevin who wanted her to release the anger, venom, and vicious self-protection mask. Now, she knew the Savior above wanted the same thing for her. Paige looked in the bulletin and grabbed the blank note card that read, "What's your baggage?" She began to write down every heavy burden that was chained to her.

Camille was already writing down her baggage. She was weighed down with personal issues. Fear of telling Karen that they were possibly sisters, and the disappointment that her father was not the superman she believed he was all of her life. Her disappointment was leading her to doubt if Benjamin was her Adam, or like her dad, too good to be true. Her work baggage was full of imbalance, and the need to work long hours to prevent her fear of failure. Just this morning Camille strapped on baggage for church hurt. Mrs. Carol gifted that piece of luggage with her ugly remarks and mean spirit. Nevertheless, she was determined to cast all these cares on the Master. According to Pastor Caine and Peter, He wanted her burdens and anxiety.

Benjamin's chained baggage was that he held other people's baggage. Pastor Caine's message was divinely inspired. Benjamin received from it that he could help carry Mrs. Carol's burden of grief by praying for her, giving her a listening ear, helping her enroll in counseling, and showing her love. However, he could not let her refusal to heal from grief become his baggage. The light bulb went off for Ben. If he continued to carry Lauren's mother's grief, he would lose his future. Ben wrote a one-liner on his baggage card, *other peoples*.

In twenty-two minutes, Pastor Caine delivered a message of deliverance. As he ministered, he started to unlock and remove the chained luggage on his person. He explained Hebrews 12:1, "Therefore, since we are surrounded by such a great cloud of witnesses, let us throw off everything that hinders and the sin that so easily entangles. And let us run with perseverance the race marked out for us."

Pastor Cain finished the sermon asking a key question.

"Have you entered the race with Christ? If you are not in the race, you must accept Jesus as your personal savior. If you are in the race, you must prepare yourself to finish the race well. A runner when racing dresses light so they may run a diligent race. We, as Christians, cannot diligently run if we are loaded with baggage. Therefore, we must cast and throw down the weights of not forgiving others, anxiety, and doubt. We must do away with sins, doing things, we know are wrong. We must look to Jesus for our help. It is not always easy to do this. Liberty Church is here to help you. We offer free counseling for individuals, couples, family, and grief counseling by licensed therapists."

Pastor Caine extended his hands toward the congregation. "The praise and worship team is coming to minister to our hearts through song. Please take your notecards and list the baggage you want to release today. Come throw it on the altar and leave it there. The elders are here to pray with you, and the spirit of Christ is here to heal you."

The praise and worship ministry began to sing Tasha Cobb's version of "Break Every Chain." The aisles of the sanctuary were filled with people eager to release their baggage and lay aside their weights and sin. Kevin, Paige, Camille, and Benjamin were among those people.

Not one of them would ever be the same again.

The Greatest Love Series

Book 2

After Church

Book 3

Dawn and Autumn

Book 4

Just Be Held

Connect with Genevieve

www.gdwoodsbooks.com

www.amazon.com/author/genevievewoods

facebook.com/Genevieve D. Woods

Book Club Questions

1. Do you think Mrs. Carol will ever get help and accept Camille and Benjamin's relationship?

2. Do you think Karen and Frankie's relationship will last?

3. How do you think Paige's past has affected her present relationship?

4. Do you think Jacob Darius (J. D.) will accept Karen and pursue a relationship with her and Nikki?

5. What do you think happened to Karen's wedding cake?

6. Do you believe Paige can ever form a cordial relationship with Kevin's mother?

7. Do you think Shayla will allow Frankie to live in peace with his new wife and family?

8. Do you think one message from a Pastor can be the answer to each couple's problems?

Made in the USA
Lexington, KY
06 March 2017